THE ADVENTURES OF
Captain
Graves

AIRSHIP 27 PRODUCTIONS

The Adventures of Captain Graves
© 2018 Thomas McNulty

Published by Airship 27 Productions
www.airship27.com
www.airship27hangar.com

Interior illustrations © 2018 Ed Catto
Cover illustration © 2018 Ted Hammond

Editor: Ron Fortier
Associate Editor: Fred Adams Jr.
Marketing and Promotions Manager: Michael Vance
Production and design by Rob Davis

ISBN-13: 978-1-946183-41-5
ISBN-10: 1-946183-41-5

Printed in the United States of America

10 9 8 7 6 5 4 3 2 1

For my beautiful wife, Jan, and to the memory of those seafaring adventurers Templeton Crocker William Beebe and Errol Flynn

THE ADVENTURES OF Captain Graves

by
Thomas McNulty

Will all great Neptune's ocean wash this blood
Clean from my hand? No, this my hand will rather
The multitudinous seas incarnadine,
Making the green one red.

—William Shakespeare, *The Tragedy of Macbeth,* act II, scene II

The bottom of the sea is cruel.

—Hart Crane, *Voyages*

Consider the subtleness of the sea; how its most dreaded creatures glide under water, unapparent for the most part, and treacherously hidden beneath the loveliest tints of azure. Consider also the devilish brilliance and beauty of many of its most remorseless tribes, as the dainty embellished shape of many species of sharks. Consider once more, the universal cannibalism of the sea; all whose creatures prey upon each other, carrying on eternal war since the world began.

—Herman Melville, *Moby Dick,* chapter 58

PROLOGUE

Honolulu, Hawaii, December 21, 1952

The man that came walking up the street was five feet eight inches tall. His crew cut gave him away as an ex-marine. His notebook gave him away as a reporter. The fact that he was a reporter was always a warning signal that someone had found him again. The man behind the beach-front Tiki bar nodded to another man near him, and then he slipped quietly into the back room. The man that took his place was tall and possessed features that spoke of a Roman ancestry.

The reporter sat at the bar and ordered a beer. He set the notebook on the bar. A silver ballpoint pen gleamed in his white shirt pocket. It was a short-sleeved shirt but the underarms were stained with sweat from the heat. Sweat also glistened on the man's brow and on his neck. He wore brown trousers and scuffed brown shoes.

"Merry Christmas." The reporter said, sipping his beer. "What is this?"

"Schlitz."

"Is that what the tourists like?"

"It's what most anyone likes. The tourists don't care what they drink."

"Do you work for Elliot Graves?"

"What's it to you who I work for?"

The reporter took another sip of beer. "I pulled the real estate papers on this place. Elliot Graves owns this fly-trap."

"You want that I should hurt you?"

The man rubbed his five o'clock shadow with his palms, ran his hand through his crew-cut hair.

"I want to know what happened to Victoria Ransom. The story will get around. These things can't be covered up. My editor knows I'm here. I'm just one guy, but there's no shortage of flat-foot reporters. Let me tell the story and I'll tell it straight."

"Mr. Graves is indisposed."

"Yeah."

The reporter finished his beer and ordered another one. They had the bar set-up outside the restaurant for the tourists that liked to drink in the shade and watch the dames on the beach. Bamboo awnings and palm trees offered shade; the tables and chairs offered the best view. When the tourists got tanked they stumbled into the restaurant and ordered dinner. But the reporter wasn't hungry. He appeared fatigued. He took his beer and moved to a table just at the edge of the beach and under a red umbrella. He drank the second beer slowly.

The beach was crowded. The sun was high and made the horizon look like molten gold. In a few hours the sky would turn into a postcard scene of reds and yellows, the palm trees silhouetted against the blistering sky, the tips of the waves gleaming like diamonds. The gleeful sound of young lovers frolicking in the sand drifted back to the tall man behind the bar.

The reporter walked down to the harbor and let his eyes roam over the ships and boats. A long line of runabouts with gleaming mahogany prows were the favorites of recreational boaters. He wanted one himself. A little four seater, with a 250 horsepower Evinrude he could take a dame out on Lake Michigan with; maybe Peggy from re-writes, or Wanda, that waitress on Division Street with the platinum hair. But Chicago was a long way away. His editor at the *Chicago Metro News*, Mort Gibson, had limited his expense account, so part of the tab was his own. Call it "vacation time," Mort had said. If the story panned out there might be a bonus. "Don't bet on it, buddy, Victoria Ransom disappeared over fifteen years ago. She's out there as fish food with Amelia Earhart. Bring 'em both back and you're a hero."

There were larger motorboats, small sailboats, fishing boats and several schooners. He had his eye on the schooners. Two of them fit the description he was looking for—a schooner with two masts—but the names were wrong. *Beachcomber* and *Darlene's Dream* didn't come close to *The Reaper's Scythe*. He wasn't surprised. *The Reaper's Scythe* was reportedly sunk off the Australian coast in 1944. It's owner, Elliot Graves, had disappeared with his ship. Still, there was something about *Beachcomber* that looked familiar.

Reporter Bill Harrison knew that Elliot Graves was alive, and he operated this Tiki Bar and worked as a fishing guide for the tourists. Graves had been the last one to see Victoria Ransom alive.

Walking up the pier, he paused a moment to enjoy the warm breeze and bright colors that were so far removed from the industrial gray of Chicago at Christmastime. He could see the blue neon sign advertising TIKI BAR and COLD BEER already glowing brightly in the fading afternoon light. The softer murmur of voices punctuated by pleasant laughter drifted out from the tables. Having already accepted that his quest wouldn't be easy, he was resigned to the fact that all of his time here would require a great deal of determination. He sighed.

Returning to the bar he ordered another beer from the tall Italian-looking bartender. The man did not look happy to see him.

"My name is Bill Harrison," He said. "I work for the *Chicago Metro News*. I was on Guadalcanal. I met a guy there named Richard Knox. He said Victoria Ransom died on an island, and that Elliot Graves was there. They were engaged before she disappeared. She was the love of his life." He set his business card on the bar. "I'm at the Honolulu Hotel. Please tell Mr. Graves I would like to speak with him."

The man took the card and slipped it into his shirt pocket without speaking. Dark eyes stared back at Harrison. "I'm not looking for trouble. I simply want the story. It has to come out sometime."

Silence greeted him. Harrison drank his beer, paid his tab, and left.

At the hotel, he showered and shaved before eating a light dinner downstairs in the adjoining restaurant. After dinner, he browsed the paperback rack in the gift shop. He had to choose carefully because of his limited budget. Twenty-five cents was a lot of his dollar to spend on a cheap pocket paperback instead of a plate of eggs, corned beef hash and a cup of coffee. He spun the rack and perused the titles: *Dragon's Island* by Jack Williamson, *Way of a Wanton* by Richard S. Prather, *Vengeance is Mine* by Mickey Spillane, *A Bullet for My Love* by Octavus Roy Cohen, *Poison in Jest* by John Dickson Carr, *A Stretch on the River* by Richard Bissell, *Wintertime* by Jan Valtin, *Her Life to Live* by Oriana Atkinson and a dozen more. Mysteries and sexy potboilers. He was on the fence between the Spillane and the Bissell, finally choosing the Spillane because word of mouth got around he was good. The paperback's back cover had four small photos of Spillane sporting a revolver. The crew-cut made Spillane look like a marine. Harrison could relate.

Back in his room, he removed a thick manila folder from his suitcase and spread out the contents on the small table near the balcony. He had the door open for the breeze. The files he had accumulated were a combination from the *Chicago Metro News* morgue files and some from his connections with the Associated Press and United Press Syndicate. He had 8x10 glossies and dozens of clippings.

Harrison studied the photographs. Elliot Graves was tall and handsome with features not unlike Tyrone Power, except for that scar beneath his left eye. The scar gave him an ominous look. He had a 1933 photograph of Graves aboard *The Reaper's Scythe* with some of the crew visible in the background. He was posing with Victoria Ransom. They were waving and smiling. Three crew members were visible in the background, but only one of them clearly. That man, Harrison was certain, was the same tall man that had just served him a beer down at the dockside Tiki Bar.

He turned his attention to Victoria Ransom. The tall, beautiful brunette was the daughter of millionaire August Ransom, founder of the Chief Tire Company, a venture that reaped him his second fortune. His first fortune was made with a trucking freight service. The Ransoms were not only wealthy, but influential. Victoria, Augusts' only child, was reportedly headstrong with a thirst for adventure. She had participated in a gold prospecting hunt in Polynesia, but had come up empty. Somewhere during this period—1932 or 1933—she had met Elliot Graves. They were inseparable for a few years, and then she disappeared.

August Ransom offered a ten million-dollar reward for her safe return, or proof that she had perished. An additional million was tacked on if her murderer were brought to justice. He didn't stop there. Six months after her disappearance, August Ransom publicly accused Elliot Graves of murder. The accusations made headlines across the country. Graves was interviewed by police detectives in San Francisco, but no charges were ever filed. Then the rumors started. Graves himself was said to have spent a fortune combing the Pacific for any sign of his lost love; others believed he knew more than he was saying. One factor was consistent in everything that Harrison had studied: few really believed that Graves was complicit in Ransom's disappearance and presumed death, but everyone agreed that he knew something he wasn't telling.

August Ransom himself believed that at the very least Graves knew something. But what? August Ransom died of a heart attack in 1942. Elliot Graves dropped out of sight two years later. Rumors about Graves circulated for years.

Then Harrison had met Richard Knox on Guadalcanal.

Guadalcanal was the part of this story he didn't like thinking about. But after the war he had read a book about Guadalcanal by Richard Tregaskis, and he wanted to be a writer, too. Tregaskis had been on that smudge of an island, and like Harrison, he was grateful to have survived. But the men that fought on Guadalcanal didn't like talking about it. Not one bit.

Even then, young as he was, he had a reputation as a bookworm and a writer. He wrote a few pieces for *Stars & Stripes*, borrowed what books he could find, but they were scarce on Guadalcanal. It was an island of death, and the images intruded upon him from time to time. The heat and the black insects on the bloated corpses of the dead Japanese soldiers. The heat and the way the lips pulled back from the teeth after the corpse had been lying out a few days, the eyes covered with insects, the bugs all over the grinning yellow teeth. The heat and the sound of the P-400s giving the Japs hell from a heavenly blue sky. The heat and the sound of the Springfield M1903 rifle, a stuttering and lethal burst repeated over and over again.

What the hell was he doing on another goddamn island?

Richard Knox had been wounded at the battle of Crocodile Creek, half his leg blown off by a shell from one of his own 75 mm howitzers. He was a goner, the only surprise being that he lasted three days, but ultimately a victim of friendly fire. Blood loss and shock had done irreparable damage to his system. Harrison encountered him as he was passing his stretcher when he reached out and asked for a smoke. He tapped out a stick from the Chesterfield pack, lit it for him and held it to his lips. He sucked on the tobacco greedily, the blue smoke cradling his head like ghostly hands. His eyes fell on the small spiral notebook stuck in his belt near his canteen.

"Take a letter, kid."

He dictated a letter and Harrison wrote it down. His was the second such letter that he had written, and he admitted at the time that he fully expected—or should he say *hoped*—that he might live long enough to get off a few final words to his family. Knox dictated his letter to his mother. It was the usual stuff, heartbreaking to talk about even now, with years providing Harrison the semblance of a cushion.

Sorry to let you down mother, and I want you to know how much I love you and sis. Always remember that, okay? That's the important part, the love. I did some good here and the guys have been swell....

Two pages like that, gutwrenching. When he was done, Knox grinned through the pain up at Harrison. "Kid, that's it. If we had more time I'd tell you about Victoria Ransom, she was a real looker, and better than Betty Grable. I saw her, kid, so I would know."

"How did you know her?" Harrison asked as he carefully folded Knox's final letter home into his shirt pocket.

"Before the war...I was a rum-runner from Singapore...into mainland China...got out of that...part of the world in time to come back...and get blown up." He coughed up a little blood and grinned again at Harrison. "Hey, Hemingway, you get the story, see? She died on an island...back in '36. Talk to Graves about her...he was in like Flynn with that dame...go'wan, Hemingway, go'wan..."

Knox was unconscious then, and he died a few hours later.

Harrison wouldn't have time to dwell on the man's enigmatic comment;

at least not for a very long time. Guadalcanal happened to him then, and by some very special miracle, he had walked away with superficial flesh wounds, and perhaps a psychic wound that might never heal. He dealt with it, and he begrudgingly accepted the applause when they pinned a few medals on him. Not as many as Audie Murphy, but enough, and after awhile he stopped talking about it.

After the war, he took night classes in writing and composition on the second floor of a small office building on Chicago's Dearborn Street. His marine corps connections put him in contact with the right people. Suddenly, he was a writer working for the *Chicago Metro News*. Harrison worked diligently. Having forgotten about Richard Knox, he was reminded of the incident some years later when his editor, Mort Gibson, wanted him to write a feature on the tenth anniversary of Amelia Earhart's disappearance. "Nothing too exploitive," Gibson had said, "but remember that Earhart and Victoria Ransom are the two greatest unsolved disappearances in our time. The public will eat it up."

It all began to fall together for him then. He was building confidence as a writer, but still longing to write something more than fluff. News reports and sports features had taken him to a certain point, and now he wanted to push himself and tell a story that had some backbone.

That night he slept fitfully. He was up before dawn and drank coffee on the hotel's veranda while watching the sky change color. He read from the Spillane paperback, and then perused the Honolulu newspapers. At noon, he checked with the front desk clerk but no messages had been left for him.

He spent the afternoon roaming about the city. Honolulu had changed. It was growing, becoming something larger than it had been prior to December 7, 1941. Had it only been eleven years? At sunset, Harrison left the hotel wearing a palm leaf button-down shirt and brown slacks. He had polished his shoes and tied them tightly as if they were stitches on his feet. He walked along the beach and studied the lavender and yellow sunset, prettier than any postcard, and uncaring of the Pacific's recent history of violence.

The city was aglow with neon. Brighter, almost defiant, Honolulu had become a place that now seemed to cherish its freedom. A popular tourist destination, primarily because of the thousands of servicemen that spoke of it so fondly to their wives.

He smoked a Chesterfield and walked into an avenue of movie theatres and bars and burlesque shows. He briefly thought he might take in a film but the long titles baffled him. *The Greatest Show on Earth* was raking in the dough, but he had seen enough circuses. Stuff like *Zombies of the Stratosphere* was incomprehensible to him, and films like *Son of Paleface* boasting a cast that included Bob Hope, Jane Russell and Roy Rogers seemed unreal and far removed from the America he had known before wartime. The Martin and Lewis comedy he had already seen in Chicago.

The bookstores were closed at this hour but the burlesque shows were open. Still, Harrison wasn't in the mood for a fan dancer in the smoky confines of a darkened room where a blue lamp illuminated a gaudy stage and teased of things that were beyond his bankroll. There was a shiny new Hudson Hornet parked on the street and Harrison admired its lines. The Hudson gleamed in the neon. It was painted a light green, and when they were new like this, a car like the Hudson was a dream. His goal was the new Chevrolet Bel Air hardtop, but a newspaperman's salary made it just out of reach. He thought he might afford the Bel Air as a good used car in a year or two, but this Hudson was giving him second thoughts. He knew it would cost more than the Bel Air. Strolling down the street and idly perusing the cars or shop windows and glittering marquees took his mind off things, but then when he glanced up the street he saw that tall man from the Tiki bar half a block away.

Harrison nearly smiled. He didn't know the man's name yet, but he was a shipmate of Elliot Graves aboard *The Reaper's Scythe*; and now he served booze in a Tiki bar owned by the enigmatic Graves. Harrison was pleased that he had stirred something up.

He made up his mind not to look back. He returned to his hotel and had a Budweiser in the bar. The bar patio opened onto a veranda that faced the sea. The breeze came in and brought with it the sound of a radio playing Don Cornell singing *I'm Yours*. The radio went on with Eddie Fisher and Johnnie Ray; Rosemary Clooney and Doris Day. He thought he could faintly hear a woman singing along. Finally, they played the Les Paul instrumental, *Meet Mr. Callaghan*, a song that Harrison liked.

Harrison was hoping he might be confronted here, so he kept his eye on the door. Keeping to himself, he managed to avoid the brunette barfly when she was making a big deal of rattling her purse when she sat two stools away from him. He didn't have to worry about her when the bar filled up and she became occupied by a businessman's overtures.

Honolulu was in full swing. The night offered promises of sex, laughter and even tears; just as the morning offered a hangover and a busted budget. Harrison had been bookish and prone to introspection since childhood. His parents bought the pulp magazines *All-Story Weekly*, *Adventure* and

Black Mask which left an impression. He was content fending for himself as long as he had a good magazine to read. Sitting in the hotel bar and thinking about Elliot Graves and Victoria Ransom he was struck by the thought that he hadn't changed in that regard. Sure, Guadalcanal had done things to him, and in that madness had come this connection to an old sailor's past, and for the first time in his life he wondered if a providential hand played a role in his actions.

Maybe I've had too much beer, he thought. He paid the tab and gave the bartender a tip. He went out on the veranda and looked at the phosphorescent waves lapping at the sand. There was a band playing swing music up the beach and amongst the strings of colored lights, he saw couples dancing gaily and he heard the pleasant sound of people laughing. He walked away from the hotel and down the beach, acutely aware of the waves whispering on his left.

Entering a crowd of revelers, he found himself in a beachfront party with young girls in sarongs doing their Dorothy Lamour act for the tourists. In the back of his mind, he was trying to figure the best angle of approach to Elliot Graves. He saw the tall Italian man at the open-air bar sitting under the colored lights and drinking a pineapple drink. He didn't appear to have seen Harrison yet, so he went around and came up behind him to slip onto the stool next to him. Before he could say anything wise, which had been his plan, the man said, "Nice try, but I had you pegged some time ago. My name is Rocco."

"Rocco." Harrison repeated. "You were a mate aboard *The Reaper's Scythe*."

"First mate. You having anything to drink?"

"What is that you're drinking?"

"Pineapple rum. I'm buying." Rocco ordered the drink and when it was sitting in front of Harrison he lit a cigarette. Harrison lit a Chesterfield and sipped his drink.

"Not bad. A little sweet for my taste."

"You're not the first to come looking for the captain." Rocco said.

Harrison nodded. "But the question is, do I get the story? Look, I'm not out to hurt anybody. I met Richard Knox on Guadalcanal. I only want to know what happened to Victoria Ransom."

"She's dead. That much I can tell you. The rest needs to come from the captain."

"If I can get that much of a statement to put the mystery to rest, then I'm done here."

"Knox must have been one of the sea bums working transport for a scoundrel named Thad Bellamy. He's dead, too."

"Knox died on Guadalcanal. I've never heard of Thad Bellamy." Harrison paused. "Look, I'm an honest man. If there's something you don't want published, then it stays with me. I'm not on a witch hunt. I'll only put as much in the paper as you want, and that's my job. Hell, if the story's that good maybe I can change all the names and make a paperback out of it."

Rocco was studying him. He nodded. "It's that good. I'll tell the captain what you said."

They finished their drinks. Harrison sensed that some type of resolution was at hand, but now he had to wait. Rocco paid the tab and then disappeared into the crowd. With nothing better to do, Harrison ordered another pineapple rum drink. The damn things grew on you, he thought.

He had another sleepless night where he tossed and turned. He was up before the sun and found himself staring at the darkened sea. After a moment, he realized that Guadalcanal was out there with the bodies of his friends. Then he realized that this same sea had a story about Victoria Ransom and Elliot Graves, and that was the story he was after. He had breakfast in the hotel restaurant when he realized he had no idea what to do next. No promises had been made. Rocco had simply stated that he would talk with Captain Graves. That was hardly an indication he was welcome.

At noon on Christmas Eve, the bellhop found him to say a message had been left at the front desk for him. He retrieved the message and stared at it a moment. It was an address on the coast. He knew the area. The real estate was being bought up by movie stars and oil executives. In twenty years the coastal homes would be worth millions.

An hour later a yellow taxi dropped him at the drive which curled up a small hill and stopped at modern ranch home that might have been designed by Frank Lloyd Wright. The lines were all even, sharp, and everything looked solid. The place was nearly surrounded by jungle although the front overlooked a cliff-side view of the Pacific. He rapped the brass door knocker fashioned after a mermaid.

The middle-aged woman that opened the door was beautiful. Although crow's feet tugged at her eyes, she was still breathtaking with smooth brown skin and bright eyes. Her black hair was laced with gray but everything about her spoke of a strong spirit, good health and intelligence. She wore tan slacks and a pearl blue short-sleeved shirt and brown slip-on shoes.

A silver necklace graced her lovely neck. The red diamonds in the silver pendant caught the light.

"You must be Mr. Harrison," she said, holding out her hand. "My name is Lani. Won't you come in? Elliot is eager to speak with you. Would you like some coffee?"

"Why yes, thank you, that's nice."

The house was expansive, comfortable, the furniture neither too old or too modern. Everything was tasteful, clean and uncluttered. The room she led him to, however, was entirely different.

Elliot Graves sat at a desk with his back to the windowed deck that overlooked the ocean. The room was cluttered with bookcases. Each shelf held too many books and journals that caused the shelves to sag. Any free wall space was adorned with framed nautical charts, paintings, documents and photographs. A Mauser rifle was propped against one bookcase. A Japanese sword against another. A sextant and compass were on his desk along with stacks of columnar paper and several leather journals. There were some clay tablets on a shelf bearing Chinese symbols, and in one corner, perched on a beautiful varnished wooden stand, sat what looked like a jade Buddha. Harrison noticed the 1911 .45 automatic on the desk as well. He had no doubt that it was loaded. Elliot Graves came around the desk, shook his hand and smiled.

"Welcome, Mr. Harrison, I'm Elliot Graves. I understand you have some questions for me?"

Graves had smiled but he was still imposing. The man was taller than Harrison had expected. He estimated six feet and five inches. The scar on his face gave him a slightly ominous appearance, but his eyes were perhaps the giveaway. They were sadder than Harrison had expected, in fact, everything about the man was taking him by surprise. His hair was nearly all gray now but his skin was still smooth. He had a deep tan.

"Why yes, and thank you for seeing me. I spoke with your man Rocco. I'd like to know what happened to Victoria Ransom."

Graves frowned and gestured to a chair. "Why don't we sit down. Lani will bring some coffee in a moment."

They sat in opposite chairs in front of the desk. Harrison was conscious of the seascape outside the window. Graves noticed his wandering gaze.

"The sea is compelling, isn't she?"

"Yes, and deadly." Harrison surprised himself by stating what was on his mind. Graves raised an eyebrow.

"I understand you knew Richard Knox on Guadalcanal. That's a rough

"But there's more...isn't there?"

deal, that island. I had friends that never came back from the Pacific. As for Victoria Ransom, she's quite dead. She died on an island called Sumtoa in the South China Sea in 1936."

"Why haven't you told anyone? You could put the mystery and speculation to rest."

"I'm afraid you don't understand. I *have* told people what happened to Victoria, it's just that nobody believes me, and for good reason. The story is too incredible to believe."

"You're right, I don't understand."

"Victoria died when the island of Sumtoa exploded in the same manner of Krakatoa in 1883. She was near a cliff and fell to her death, and of course the island sank into a lava flow. Her body could never be recovered. I reported all of this dutifully to her father, but he never believed it."

It was his tone of voice that gave it away. Harrison decided to gamble.

"But there's more to it than that isn't there? There must be some reason why the full story hasn't been told."

Graves leveled his gaze on Harrison and for one long uncomfortable moment the two men stared at each other.

"All right." Graves said finally. "That's the official story, and the one you print. Keep my present location out of the paper. Since you're a writer you might appreciate this." Graves stood up, went around his desk and set his palm on a large leather journal. "It's all in here. I wrote it down just a few weeks later."

At that moment Lani returned with a tray of coffee. She poured each of them a cup and set the tray on the desk. Her smile warmed the room.

"We'll need some bourbon, too." Graves said. Lani nodded.

"Bourbon?"

"You'll see." Graves said. He picked up the journal. "Let's sit out here in the sun with our coffee and bourbon."

They sat at a metal-framed table painted white. The air was warm and the surf crashed at the rocks far below them. Lani brought the bourbon and Graves poured a touch into each coffee cup.

"Start reading, and then I'll explain some things when you're finished."

Harrison opened the book. It was a handwritten journal with the name *The Reaper's Scythe* embossed in gold on the leather-bound cover. Harrison read a few pages and stopped. He took a long pull from his bourbon laced coffee. He read a few more pages then drained his coffee cup. He was sweating.

"We have plenty of bourbon." Graves said. His eyes were luminescent.

His voice was strong. Harrison understood why his crew were devoted to him. The man's very aura commanded your attention.

Harrison sipped more bourbon laced coffee and continued reading...

ONE

From the Journal of Captain Elliot Graves
Singapore, August, 1936

Last night I dreamed that Victoria Ransom's corpse floated to the surface of the South China Sea, her mouth clotted with kelp, her eyes shining like two silver coins. She was emotionless and unrepentant; a trinket the sea had given back for some beachcomber to find on a fog-shrouded morn. Her sheer nightgown clung to her obscenely, outlining every once delectable curve.

Perhaps this is not a tale that I should tell, but I am compelled out of compassion for lost friends to record these events. The events of which I am writing transpired just weeks past and I will endeavor to get as much down on paper as I can.

One morning quite early, and after a night of too much whiskey, I took my breakfast with Rocco in the salon. We ate our eggs and bacon silently, washing it down with that bad Chinese coffee we'd picked up the week before.

"We need some British coffee." I ventured at last.

"Brazilian." Rocco argued. "And forget American coffee. You Americans are intent on stuffing everything into a tin can."

"Beggars can't be choosers."

"Aye, Captain, and beggars we'll never be."

"Your point is well taken."

After breakfast, I went to my cabin where I spent an hour reviewing some correspondence and notes on our latest finds. Having departed the Cook Islands, we thought to rest for several weeks and take in supplies from the Singapore markets. We found the place teeming with communists and cocky Brits who had forgotten they remained a minority. Strolling through the narrow streets where laundry was hung to dry like rows of tattered flags, I briefly reveled in the scents of freshly cooked meats and fishes that charred on steel grates for low prices in every corner shop for blocks at a time. The sea air was strong enough to dispel the smell of the unwashed poor, all of whom stared at us with uncomprehending eyes as we made our way like conquerors through the sweating crowds.

I sent several telegrams from the British consulate's office to New

York. We had procured a multitude of photographic documents and sea specimens in sealed jars that had been bought and paid for in advance by the good board of directors of the Natural History Museum. Additionally, our two motion picture cameras had documented various aspects of our expedition, which would go far in promoting interest in the museum. A great deal of our footage would be sold as newsreel filler or stock footage for the big movie studios in Los Angeles, sub-contracted through the Natural History Museum. I take my money where I find it.

Late in the afternoon, we found ourselves eating fresh lobster and potatoes in a sea-front restaurant that catered to the British. The place was really a dive with the colorful name The Angry Baboon Saloon. Favoring the British is natural for me given the fact that my lineage can be traced to the age of Cornwall. My ancestors, perhaps not unjustly, disturbed by the British Commonwealth's Stamp Act, retaliated with a War of Independence wherein my relatives soundly routed the Brits. These tales of the Revolutionary War had inspired me as a child, and perhaps were indirectly responsible for my troubles. I appear to seek battlegrounds across the globe. All the same, my forebears had family in England and even today I'm in contact with various cousins. Our political differences aside, family is family. It's quite simply good manners to avoid any mention of King George III's cruelties when in the presence of a British military officer. And much safer.

This, however, was not the thinking of Rocco Salventi, first mate aboard The Reaper's Scythe. Being a hot-headed Italian he often found himself flapping his gums with the skill of a stage orator. I can imagine Rocco during the age of Julius Caesar, pontificating before the throngs, his eyes shining with enthusiasm. When his wind is up, he is rather formidable. The rest of the time, he is simply dangerous.

The day was meant for relaxation while purchasing supplies before setting sail. I was accompanied by Rocco along with the kid Johnny Turner, ship's mate Dusty Smith, Doc Casper Caspian and Edgar Bumpassé, our cook. Edgar, being rotund and exceedingly jolly, was also finicky when it came to our grub. Claiming lineage to cattle drive cooks in the old west who rode with gunslingers like Hank Benteen, Edgar fancied himself a chef of the same skill level as those Parisians who made their names with soufflés one finds on the menu of New York hotels. Johnny Turner had but joined our crew that season; a brash but likeable young man with a taste for Robert Louis Stevenson and big dreams of finding treasure. Had I but known what treasure he would indeed find, and the consequences thereof, the results might have been different for him. But hindsight is a form of torture. Dusty Smith was lanky and strong, red-headed with freckles and an Oklahoma drawl. Doc Caspian hailed from Virginia and possessed the calmest nature of all our shipmates. A kind and gentle soul, he perused the world over a pair of spectacles that seemed forever perched at the tip of his nose. Aboard ship waited Badoo, a black sailor of Zulu origin but who spoke perfect English. Badoo was a fierce warrior and preferred the solitude of a lonely ship when the crew went ashore. There was never any worry that our ship would be invaded because Badoo could fight like twelve men.

These were my crew, enough to operate a schooner, and enough to find trouble, which had been our privilege from time to time.

Rocco had engaged a British sergeant in conversation, and soon they became loud. We had finished eating and Rocco was enjoying a cigar. He stood at the bar and I knew from his tone that a fight was about to begin. Doc, Johnny, Edgar and Dusty watched with bemusement. Rocco seldom lost, and I didn't believe the Brit could take him, but there was always the chance. We eyed the other Brits to assess any interference level, eager to avoid an all-out brawl. They were nonchalant, which is a deceptive habit among the British. We were alert to any movement, and then the fight was underway.

I don't recall the exact point of contention, and men with a bellyful of whiskey don't require that much encouragement. I heard Rocco say, "Your mother's loose corset is well known in Piccadilly. I've had a go at her myself, but only after imbibing for six days." And there was a comment about her Wellington's being employed as a commode for the sailors lined up next to her brass bed rail. The sergeant threw the first punch, a nice right cross that skimmed Rocco's chin with enough force to snap his head back. This was going to be interesting because the sergeant was fast.

Rocco landed what should have been a haymaker, a right cross of his own that connected with a square jaw but with little effect. The Brit shook is head and snorted like a bull. His left uppercut caught Rocco mid-ships and he doubled. A fist came flying at his head and I thought we might see history in the making as Rocco tumbled. But that never came to pass.

Rocco charged. They were a tangle of slamming fists and lashing legs, two gladiators from a past age playing a deadly game. It was a terrific fight. During the melee, I had a vague sense of awareness of a lithe figure entering through the sunlit doorway, and a few whistles as if the men were admiring a dame, but I was too preoccupied to turn my head for a better look. When it was over the sergeant was flat out on the floor, his companions eyeing us warily. The danger passed, and they hauled the sergeant to his feet. After reviving him, Rocco congratulated his earnest opponent for a grand fight. They were about to enjoy a whiskey together when a voice interrupted the scene and forever changed my life.

"You're Elliot Graves. I need your help."

The woman that stood before me was five feet and nine inches, a long mane of raven black hair pulled away from the features of a stunning beauty. I immediately mistook her for a Polynesian. She wore slacks and a button-down shirt, which was wise given the feminine curves that could not be disguised by even such conservative clothing. I was dumbfounded, but only momentarily. Her eyes were green, an unusual feature among any islanders. Her skin was a light brown with a creamy complexion and unmarked by any of the usual popular cosmetics. She was naturally beautiful, imminently desirable, and I could not stop staring at her. She may have blushed as I sized her up.

"My name is Malulani Kawena, but my friends call me Lani. My father is Joseph Kawena, the chief of anthropology at the College of Honolulu."

"I see. And how can I help you?"

I was conscious of the fact that my whiskey glass, still clutched in my right hand, had been tilted as I rose from my chair. The whiskey was sloshed over my knuckles, just as it had been sloshed over my tongue. I set the glass down and used a handkerchief to clean myself up. For some reason I didn't wish to appear unclean in front of this woman.

"You know Victoria Ransom. I think my father is with her, although I'm not sure. I do know they're connected somehow, and I need to find them."

This took me by surprise. "That's yesterday's news, sister." I said, perhaps a bit more gruffly than I intended. "Victoria and I are last year's gossip. We've gone our separate ways, and I have no idea where she is."

"But I do," she added quickly. "She's on the island of Sumtoa in the south China Sea. There's an active volcano on the island, and she has taken my father there with his private papers. I believe she has kidnapped my father."

This incredible piece of news silenced all talk in the room, at least among any of those that understood English. Doc Caspian, bless his heart, chose that moment to speak up. "Perhaps the young lady will be more comfortable talking about such matters aboard ship." Doc said. "And I do believe a good meal with some wine might be appropriate."

"I have some fresh potatoes," Edgar interjected. "Some fresh vegetables, too. I can prepare a feast."

Dusty and Johnny were wide-eyed and fortunately remained silent.

"You'll take me then?" she asked. "I can fetch my belongings and be ready in a few hours."

"Hold on, I haven't agreed to anything. Of course what you're saying is interesting, but *The Reaper's Scythe* is a research vessel contracted for scientific studies."

"You don't understand; the emeralds and red diamonds and the gold jewelry alone are unlike anything from any museum..."

Doc was on his feet. Rocco, having heard the conversation, slid up next to Lani and said roughly, "Let's go outside."

I glanced around the saloon cum restaurant. In addition to the Brits there were multiple seamen and unsavory types, all of whom were watching Lani fixedly. The Pandora's box had been opened although we didn't know the extent of the trouble this would cause. Lani didn't object as we hustled her out.

"Johnny, Dusty, keep a sharp eye now."

My men knew the routine, the only difference being that our caution involved the life of a rather beautiful woman. We walked at a leisurely pace and headed down to the harbor where *The Reaper's Scythe* was plainly visible at anchor. From Keppel Harbor, we could see Sentosa island. Beyond that, the sea was a glittering expanse of blue just a shade darker than the sky where gulls circled on the warm wind, their cries echoing forlornly above the piers and docks.

"Listen," I said, "all of this talk about jewels and gold can make you a target. More than a few of those men back there heard what you said, and English isn't as uncommon as you might think. You'll have to be careful."

Her face revealed her sadness and I desperately wanted to see her smile.

"I understand. I'm so sorry to impose on you like this. I thought because you knew Victoria Ransom you might help. I don't have anyone else. I came here on my own, but..." She hesitated, looking about fearfully. "Well, it's been difficult."

How could I resist her? "All right, now, how about this. Come aboard and we'll go over the charts. I've heard of Sumtoa Island but I can't place it. I have charts that will get us a good bead on the place. We have a little time and it's possible we can take a look. I'm not promising anything, because we need to look at those charts."

Her face brightened and I felt better just seeing the hope in her eyes.

"I'll get my things and meet you here in a few hours."

"Let me send Johnny and Dusty along," I offered. "Singapore is full of surprises. Where are you staying?"

"A place called The Kowloon Hotel. It's about a mile from here."

I looked at Johnny and Dusty and naturally they were eager to accompany her. Both of them had Colt automatics under their lightweight coats, which we all wore for the solitary purpose of appearing unarmed, which we never were. In a short while this precaution born from experience would save us yet again. The world, and the Far East especially, are simply not safe havens for Americans.

They went off quickly, and Johnny was already trying to impress her with some funny remarks. Doc looked at me and said sarcastically, "We have some time, do we?"

Once aboard *The Reaper's Scythe* I cleaned myself up and put on a clean shirt. Then I began poring through some old navigation charts and maps, all in preparation of impressing Lani Kawena. She was very much on my mind, but she had brought up a sore subject…Victoria Ransom.

Some preparatory remarks regarding Miss Ransom are in order, and I do not like thinking about her. But since this tale involves her I need to offer a slight history of our relationship. I met Victoria in 1932 on Cook Island. Hers was one of many well-publicized prospecting expeditions in the South Pacific, and after her failure to turn up an ounce of gold, she hosted a party. I was invited simply because my ship lay at anchor in the harbor. I took it as an opportunity to walk the rolling swells out of my knees and find the ground again; this, being every sailor's prerogative, often leads restless men into trouble.

Victoria was quite a dame. She was beautiful and talkative, and when she spoke she put on a clipped no-nonsense chatter like those Hollywood broads in the movies. Her rapid-fire euphemisms flung across the room like confetti. She reminded me of a better version of Bette Davis and Kay Francis. Far better, and far more beautiful.

Perhaps this is the way I should remember her, chattering innocuously while holding a glass of champagne in one hand and posing with a cigarette that she only pretended to smoke. Her tight dress clung to her full figure, leaving nothing to the imagination as she reveled in the attention. Here was a Siren of the sea, flung up from the depths to satiate a thirsty sailor's appetite. I wanted her very badly, and I made up my mind to have her.

To say this bluntly seems pornographic, but I did know her, and very well. And I knew the blackness in her soul and the greed that worked at her like a cancer. I knew her until she died with her skull shattered across a storm-lashed escarpment of rocks, her blood turning the sea red. I know, too, the souls that she destroyed, and having known them is a grief that

I cannot escape, nor will their ghosts let me alone. Anger grips me, and I cannot wish that she suffered more than she did, for those lives that were lost possessed more value than any treasure that she sought.

Victoria Ransom.

A name written across the page that made headlines; a smiling celebrity, daughter of a millionaire. She conquered me in bed, but not at sea.

As time went on, I learned of her true nature. She sought the spotlight so fervently, always at the expense of others. Her addiction to diamonds and gold was unnatural, and would prove her undoing. We had nothing in common outside of our mutual physical attraction. The newspapers made more of our relationship than truly existed. Of course, she was quite angry when I cut her off, but she quickly found other men to conquer. One of them, Thad Bellamy, would come to a bad end.

I have committed an injustice, I think, in offering such a fragment on Victoria Ransom, but seekers of gossip can always read those old magazine stories and feel duly enlightened. For my part, my anger is too rich, and the act of writing these words has broken the pencil in my own hand.

Badoo, having disappeared the moment we returned to the ship, suddenly reappeared with a cryptic comment.

"I heard an old sea shanty echo on the wind."

He had silently entered my cabin where I stood poised over the charts. I hadn't heard him enter. I glanced up at him but, as usual, he was stoic.

"I suppose you're going to tell me it's from the Flying Dutchman?"

"I don't know."

"Well, what do you think it is then?"

"A bad omen. We need to pull up anchor and set sail."

"Where would we go? Do you have a destination in mind where we won't be hearing songs on the wind?"

"The sea breeze can work like a mirage. Under certain weather conditions we can see the reflection of things not normally visible, or we can hear things from afar, carried to us in a sky full of screaming gulls."

I went to the cabinet and retrieved a decanter, unstopped it, and poured us both a stiff two knuckles of brandy. We drank it down. Badoo showed not the slightest reaction.

"In a little while a young woman will board the ship. We'll be setting sail on the morning tide." I said. "Her presence here will determine our next destination."

"She isn't coming."

"I beg your pardon?"

"Look at the time."

I looked at the small German-made clock ticking on the desk. Two hours had passed. I had been so involved in studying the nautical charts that I had lost track of time. Badoo was right. Johnny and Dusty were an hour overdue. Something was wrong. Johnny and Dusty were never late.

"Doc mentioned it to me," Badoo said. "Then I heard the echo on the wind."

"I see."

Badoo followed me onto the dock where I found Rocco watching the horizon from the bowsprit.

"Did you hear something, too?" I asked.

Rocco frowned. "No, but he did." He said, gesturing at Badoo. "I don't like it when he hears things on the wind. Remember what happened when we were down near Queensland?"

I nodded. "All right. Tell Doc and Edgar to stay here with Badoo. You and I will go get them."

Rocco grinned. He couldn't help himself. The man lived for adventure. Perhaps we all did, at least at the time. That is all changed now. I returned to my quarters.

There are times that we find ourselves anchored in harbors that are so tranquil in the morning that I find it difficult to issue a command for departure. The sunlight shatters across the flat surface of the water and winks at us like beckoning spirits. This is in opposition to the sunsets where the horizon turns orange and the waves turn blood-red as if the jugular of some mighty beast were bleeding out here among the solitude of beaches and faraway ports. Given the opportunity, I might one day decide that a beachcomber's life is my true calling, providing, of course, that our treasure seeking ventures gather us enough capital to live comfortably in solitude. I have never tired of a sky as blue and seemingly as fragile as a bird's egg; or a line of palm tees whose fronds wave gently in a tropical breeze. There would I be; a captain of the Tiki Bar living as some anonymous caterer proffering rum drinks to the tourists, all my turmoil behind me at last. I would be grateful should it be so. Perhaps one day it shall.

But on this day I was forced once again to remove my Colt .45 from its holster and disassemble it for cleaning. I soaked the springs and parts in a saucepan filled with oil before scrubbing them clean. My fingers darkened from the gunpowder and grime that had accumulated so quickly in the barrel. I had cleaned this gun only a few months previously but my earthbound difficulties manifest themselves each time I go ashore. Still, there is no profit in seafaring for the benefit of my eyes alone.

When I reassembled the gun, I pulled back the slide and then snapped it back in place. The metallic sound was reassuring to me. After loading the clip, I slammed it into the grip and eased it into my shoulder holster.

Rocco was waiting for me on the deck.

TWO

None of us were strangers to Singapore. Sometimes in the late afternoon, just as the sun begins to set, a band plays in the courtyard of an old hotel. And as the light slides along the stucco walls and ancient bricks, a feeling of warmth seems to spread out and touch everyone for just a little while. It appears as if suddenly the barbarians had learned to play musical instruments, and a civilization had risen from the mud and heat and squalor. The music is somehow soothing, and although the band is not as skilled as those one might find in the swank hotels of New York and Chicago, one can easily imagine falling in love while the band plays on, or at the very least going down with your ship. You get sucked in and complacent, and the music is grand and tugs at your heartstrings. We were the type of men that quietly sipped our whiskey and went along with the fantasy, a .45 tucked snugly in a shoulder harness under our arms, the clip full with brass slugs.

The blood red sunset makes a postcard picture, but when the shadows stretch into a long patch of sunlight on the cobbled street, Singapore slowly transforms into a city of forbidden and suddenly unleashed desire. Sex and money are the only captains of commerce and industry. There is nothing else; there are no pleasant diversions. Singapore is a city of many scents, not the least of which being the scent of food cooking. Suffice it to say that during earlier trips I had mistakenly sampled certain delicacies only to suffer gastrointestinal pain that was nearly fatal. We discovered that many a shipboard dog, let loose for exercise by the visiting merchant seaman, would suddenly go missing.

Singapore is also a city where murder is commonplace. The need to eat, this simple act of acquiring nourishment, is as powerful as the desire for sex and money. It is all tied together. No fancy boys can walk safely down an alley in that faraway port; no timid professor in tweed will last but minutes in any alley where the painted women beckon from hidden doorways. This was not a city where a girl as beautiful as Lani Kawena could hope for safe passage.

The hot night was filled with stars and the steady hum of people and traffic. Occasionally an automobile backfired. A rickshaw swept past us, the runner chattering in a sing-song voice as we made our way to Lani's hotel. I feared we were already too late.

The Kowloon turned out to be a flea-bag operation, not really a hotel. It was the type of place an unsuspecting tourist on a tight budget might stay at great peril to his health. The building was a long ranch-style frame with but twelve rooms. The proprietor was a thin and agitated man who waved his skinny brown arms and told us to "Go away!" between rows of yellow teeth. Lani's room was empty except for her luggage.

Rocco, being alert to his surroundings, was pointing up a dark alley.

"They went up here," he indicated.

"How do you know?"

We heard Lani scream, and then curse.

"Never mind."

The darkness was impenetrable because of the squalid buildings pressing in on each side and obliterating the little light that existed. Occasionally the yellow glow through a curtained window helped guide our way. We could hear the patter of boots on the dirt path, and muffled voices or grunts.

Suddenly there was a great struggle as we turned a corner with our guns drawn. A men yelped in pain. Thirty feet ahead of us, I saw Lani twist about and bite fiercely at a man's wrist. Howling, he slapped her hard across the face, knocking her into the dirt. Before I could fire, a shot rang out that clipped the wall near me. I dodged as a shower of dirt and splinters flew off the wall. Rocco had disappeared; I believe rushing forward.

Lani jumped to her feet and ran.

She disappeared with the speed of a gazelle before I could shout. In the half-light of a nearby window I saw three men chase after her, but not before firing their revolvers in my direction. The flying lead was enough to keep us immobile and counting the seconds through clenched teeth. The alley sloped upward and twisted off into a thousand alleys and side-streets. Death lurked in every pool of shadows; and every yellow spill of light from a lamp or window was an invitation for an ambush. Rocco rejoined me looking perturbed.

Cautious, perhaps too eager to engage our unseen enemies in battle, we proceeded intent on destroying our adversaries and bringing Lani to safety. Step by step we traversed the long dark alley. Presently we came to an intersection. Such is the nature of Singapore that its citizens remain aloof to problems or activities that are of no direct concern. So it was that a midnight call girl stood brazenly in the glow of an oil lamp that hung in the doorway of a corrugated and lopsided building that teetered precariously into the darkness. Her cigarette smelled of marijuana and her glazed lavender eyes spoke of lost dreams and the angry reality of the tropic night. Upon seeing us, she opened her mouth and chittered as if attempting to laugh. Her cruel smile revealed broken teeth. She made an obscene gesture and we moved past her swiftly.

We had entered a section of the city where Singapore's lucrative commerce was on display. An old turbaned man stood at a cart overflowing with silks of all sizes and colors. A food peddler had displayed all manner of tropical fruits and nuts on a table where the insects hovered in the glow of his lamps like an army awaiting the command to attack.

With each step we took, I sensed that unfriendly eyes marked our passage.

Ahead of us we heard shouting as Johnny and Dusty emerged from the shadows. Dusty fired his automatic, the Colt bucking in his hand, the flame belching from the muzzle like a dragon's breath. A man squealed in pain and a body thumped to the ground. Rocco shouted to them and they waved us on. I came up next to Dusty and looked at the man he had shot. The body was still twitching, the ugly little .38 still clutched in his dirty hands.

Both Dusty and Johnny looked beat to a pulp. Dusty had a fat lip.

"They took us by surprise," Dusty said. "The little greasy monkeys wanted Lani pretty bad. There's three more and they went down that alley."

A glance down the alley revealed only darkness.

A man cursed at us from the darkness.

"That's a Polynesian dialect," I translatged the curse. "We've been encouraged to visit hell." My Polynesian was only passable for modest, short conversations, but I knew enough to understand the gist of it. "Dusty, you and Johnny stay here and keep them pinned down. Rocco and I will go around to find another way in."

I thought the alley was a dead end and we had them in a tight place. We didn't know if Lani was in the same alley or if she had gotten out.

Rocco and I circled around to the next street eyeing the rooftops. I had it in mind to go over and drop in behind them. At the very least we should be able to attack from above and find out if Lani was in that alley. We found a drainpipe but it wouldn't hold our weight. Rocco found a dozen fruit crates and stacked them like steps. We were able to clamber onto a shed, and a windowsill for a foothold. Just reaching the rooftop with our fingertips, we hauled ourselves up. I could see the bay down on my left, the lights of the ships twinkling in the darkness.

Apparently one of kidnappers had the same idea. No sooner had we started across the rooftops when a figure appeared from behind a chimney and opened fire. A .38 slug whammed into a corrugated doorway and ricocheted into the muggy night.

Rocco fired once but his bullet whined off into the air. The shooter had dodged into the rippling rooftop shadows. We split up and circled around. I was coming at the shooter from the left. I saw him almost immediately crouched near an open transom. I could hear voices coming from inside the building. Rocco, coming from the other side, was barely visible to me although the shooter was looking in Rocco's direction. I didn't hesitate and I shot the man on the rooftop. The crack of my automatic sent the voices down inside the building to chattering loudly. Rocco joined me and we dragged the body away from the transom and looked down.

That was when I heard Dusty shout "Hey you!" followed by the snapping yowl of a revolver. Rocco and I dropped through the transom and hit the ground with a thud. It was only about a twenty-foot drop but we hit the floor hard. Then we were up and crashing into a hallway lit by a solitary yellow ceiling bulb. Flies swarmed in the stifling air. It was an old building, its original intention long forgotten, but now occupied by ignorant citizens; the poor, uneducated populace of Singapore. We passed several rooms with the doors open. There was no furniture, just clothes and blankets and some baskets, and tons of filth. The rooms and hallways were freely used as a commode. The stench was almost unbearable. We passed several overweight, sullen eyed women with babies held to their naked breasts.

We found Dusty at the end of a long hall. He gestured for us to remain silent and pointed at an open doorway. We gathered from his hectic gesturing that either Lani was inside or some of our attackers, possibly both. Johnny appeared and we were all together again. I sensed this was about to play out and I prayed we could extract Lani without injury.

I dodged through the doorway. Lani had been stripped naked and tied to a chair. Her clothes lay in a bundle near her chair. A man was preparing to torture her with a small knife. My Colt barked and the bullet shattered

A .38 slug...ricocheted into the muggy night..

his skull. Unfortunately, some blood splattered across Lani. Rocco came in and moved to the right. Another man, having seen us, fired his revolver wildly before dashing into another room. Rocco followed him. Dusty and Johnny came in and spread out behind me. Three men at a table playing cards rose up with guns and knives. Their bullets whizzed and snapped in the air. I was firing and rolling to the side just as Dusty and Johnny opened up on them.

Death is an ugly business. I recall with clarity the wide-eyed look of terror on Lani's face. They hadn't gagged her, and I was surprised that she didn't scream. The men screamed, however. They screamed and begged for mercy in their native tongue or in fractured English as our bullets tore them apart. The room echoed with gunfire and the sound of full-metal jacketed rounds shattering bone. Their blood ran in rivulets on the rotten floorboards. They lay twitching and dying as we heard Rocco's gun bark again and again.

I untied Lani and handed her the clothes. She dressed silently, her lips tight, her features grim. Rocco came back into the room without speaking. He simply nodded. It was almost over.

"We're going back to my ship." I said. "We can pick up your luggage on the way"

She gently placed her hand on my arm. "I'm so sorry."

"Hell, nothing to it." I said, trying to sound nonchalant. "You have a lot of spirit. The main thing is that you're not injured."

Rocco and I took the lead and Dusty and Johnny watched our backs. The five of us made our way out of that hellhole of a building. By the time we reached the street, I thought I was half-mad from the flies. We had left those flies something to feast on. I wished them well.

It was now late and nothing about Singapore resembled civilization. We had entered hell; a demonic Babylon of sin, degradation and death. Lani, I'm certain, made note of the fact that we never put our guns down. In fact, we re-loaded. I pressed fresh rounds into the clip and smacked it back in place. She observed all of this without protest.

Perhaps returning to the Kowloon Hotel for Lani's luggage was a poor decision. I may have been attempting chivalry when caution was the appropriate reaction.

They were waiting for us at the Kowloon Hotel.

Thinking about it now, I can see the flaw in my actions. Of course, I wanted to please her. A woman needed her personal belongings with her on a trip such as this. She was a long way from home. Dusty said, "Do you want Johnny and me to go in for the luggage?"

"No," I said, "we'll all go, and then to the ship."

We went in together in standard formation—Rocco and I went first followed by Lani. Dusty and Johnny had our backs. We had the luggage and had entered the hall. We saw men further down the hall, all crowded together. We pushed Lani into a room and started shooting. The fact that we opened fire first took them by surprise. A man's head turned into a geyser of blood and brains from a .45 slug. We hit the ground as a volley of gunfire raked through the room. The bullet holes made a sweeping pattern across the thin walls. The air was filled with dust.

Rocco kicked a door open and we went into another room. It was a bathroom with no way out. We backtracked, and paused to fire at the men trying to crowd into the doorway. We could hear Dusty and Johnny firing in the hall. Men were screaming.

I am not certain if I can convey the pandemonium that ensued. What saved us being the fact that Dusty and Johnny had immediately dispatched the three men that had come in behind them. Unknown to us, Dusty and Johnny then attacked the men following us into that other room. With Rocco and me firing from the bathroom the other men died in the doorway. The sound of gunfire was deafening. When it was over, I had one cartridge left. Rocco's gun was empty. Dusty had two cartridges left and Johnny's gun was likewise empty.

The fact that none of us were injured is something of a miracle. We had the luggage and our lives. Lani looked shaken but to her credit, there was no breakdown, no tears. She appeared resolute.

The trip to *The Reaper's Scythe* was uneventful. We made it to the harbor and rowed our dinghy back to the ship. With the rowboat hoisted again onto the deck, we made preparations to sail. We'd had enough of Singapore. I stood on the deck in the darkness and looked out at the twinkling lights of Singapore and glad to be rid of her.

But at the time I had no idea what we were sailing into.

THREE

This is as much a tale of the sea as it is a tale of island life; it is a tale of a vanishing people and their now lost civilization. Modern society has a long reach, and it touches those faraway places of the Pacific just as easily as it touches the sprawling suburbs of Los Angeles or San Francisco.

The Reaper's Scythe nosed her way through a phosphorescent sea, rocking lazily in a mild swell. Being at sea is something I cannot adequately describe. Perhaps it takes a novelist to convey the images and emotion that mesh to form this sensation of destiny I experience whenever I set sail. To be at sea is something splendid for we have a new adventure before us. The seas round the world are more than salt water. This is a place where ghosts whisper from across the endless waters and where beneath the surface are creatures yet to be seen by mankind. That we might glimpse them—nay, let me correct myself—that we would barely survive our encounter with a denizen of the sea's underworld is but a miracle I cannot validate. My word on this matter is on these pages. That is all the evidence I have.

Dawn broke and we had set a course to some small islands in the South China Sea. We still had specimens to collect for the Natural History Museum in New York. That I was intent on fulfilling the terms of my contract appears incredible given the events that followed.

Edgar made us all a fantastic flapjack breakfast that included scrambled eggs and fresh vegetables. We had enough supplies for about two weeks and Edgar was in his glory. Lani thanked him profusely and offered her assistance in the kitchen. This offer elicited a raised eyebrow from Edgar who controlled every aspect of our meals. Still, Lani was persuasive as all beautiful women can be, and Edgar consented to allow her to help with some of his cooking.

As the opportunity presented itself, I engaged Lani in a conversation regarding her statements in The Angry Baboon Saloon.

"You had mentioned emeralds, red diamonds and gold jewelry. How did such treasures get onto Sumtoa Island?"

"They're native to Sumtoa," She said. "A tribe of Polynesians have lived there for fifty years."

"That doesn't seem quite right." I said. "A volcanic island is generally not associated with diamonds or gold and certainly not red diamonds or emeralds. The majority of the landscape should be volcanic rock."

"But there are no natural laws that preclude precious stones or even gold. I agree it seems far-fetched, but something sparked my father's interest, and now your friend Victoria Ransom is after the treasure."

When Lani said *friend* her tone of voice changed. I stared at her a moment.

"She's not my friend. Our relationship was a mistake. I have no interest in that woman."

"I see. I didn't mean to offend you."

"Red diamonds are exceedingly rare." I said, changing the subject. "I'm not sure I understand the difference between red diamonds and rubies."

"A red diamond is precisely that," Lani explained, "a piece of carbon, a diamond, not a ruby, but tinted red by nature. Red diamonds come in various shades of red, some with a purple tint. It is the rarest gemstone in the world, but apparently my father discovered a place where they can be found in profusion."

"I remember reading that only about two dozen high quality red diamonds have ever been found."

"That was true until recently. A red diamond has a value that exceeds any other diamond, and if their colors, shape, and lack of blemishes are all good then you can well imagine what this discovery will mean."

"I understand. It would change the market and cause a diamond rush similar to a gold rush."

"And because a red diamond is valued higher than any other gemstone the effect would be tremendous."

"Just a small red diamond can make a man a millionaire several times over, right?"

"That's right," Lani said, "and my father knows this. I fear for him, Mr. Graves. I fear that Victoria Ransom is not an honorable person, and I've heard that some of her associates have shady backgrounds."

At this statement, she blushed and broke eye contact with me. I ventured to turn the conversation in a different direction.

"What do you know about the people that live on Sumtoa?"

"As I mentioned, I believe they're Polynesian," she said, once again looking at me. "But my father wasn't certain. They speak a fractured, adaptive version of the Polynesian language."

I showed Lani the map and explained our route. We were scheduled to make stops on some small islands to obtain museum samples and our arrival at Sumtoa was dependent on the speed in which we worked. Lani was satisfied, and grateful for the help we were offering.

We had several cameras on board, along with an ample supply of film. I offered Lani the opportunity to help photograph our specimens. We had three days of sailing before our first stop; a layover on a small atoll. She was pleased, and eager to help.

We settled into our usual shipboard routine, but I admit that having Lani aboard *The Reaper's Scythe* stirred emotions in me that had been dormant for some time. Ship's mate's Johnny Turner and Dusty Smith were certainly aware of Lani; and even the ever impassive Badoo was caught stealing a glance in her direction now and again. Only Doc Caspian, Rocco and Edgar appeared nonchalant.

Thinking of them now, I am proud of my crew, and any grief I feel at losing some of them is a curse upon Victoria Ransom. A curse upon her spirit should it roam the seven seas as I suspect it does.

Lani spent the next several days experimenting with the camera. We had a photographer's dark room set-up with the chemicals and supplies needed for developing our film, and Rocco gave Lani a few lessons. She was quite adept at photography, and I marveled over her prints.

Our job collecting marine life specimens coincided with the photographic record of our travels that suddenly was being handled by Lani. Her involvement took some of the work load off Rocco and myself, in fact, we came to rely on Lani in many ways. Our first stop was a small series of uncharted atolls that brought us shells from their dark sandy beaches, and a few modest samples of coral reef. It is a little known fact that due to sudden volcanic eruptions, such atolls appear and disappear with some regularity in the Pacific as often as they do in the Atlantic. So it is that steam freighters riding the trade routes will happen upon such atolls only to discover them missing on the return trip.

The seas are but a living creature; molded by fate, home to unfathomable denizens of the deep, treacherous and uncaring for the plight of mankind.

Seven days out we encountered a small island of approximately three hundred yards in any direction. The center was a tangle of thin palm trees and underbrush. The beach was pure white sand, gleaming around the island like a cake decoration. Here was such a place that buccaneers might once have left a shipmate stranded for some infraction of their piratical code.

I studied the island through my binoculars for the better part of an hour as we circled it. Curious, Lani came and stood by me, her gaze held by the swaying palms in the distance.

"Will we go ashore?" she asked at length.

"Yes, I think so. I've been watching for any sign of life, especially animals, but all I see are gulls."

"Is there any danger then?"

"Probably, and if so it would be snakes. We've encountered snakes in the damndest places out here, usually poisonous, so we'll have to be careful."

"I might want to swim to that beach. Do you think it will be all right?"

"Once we get ashore you can swim in, but I want to check the place out first. We'll bring the camera, too."

She seemed happy with that, so I informed the men we would reconnoiter on the beach. Johnny, Dusty and Rocco prepared the longboat and we set out. Using a gasoline operated outboard motor we made good time under the blazing sun. There is something choice in approaching a virgin beach for the first time, its sands unmarked by any human. There is always an expectancy and thrill as we set foot upon such a faraway paradise, leaving our own footprints for nature to wash away later with the tides.

We ventured about for an hour before waving for Lani to swim ashore. The sight that greeted us was startling, but not unwelcome. Lani, dressed in a blue two-piece bathing suit was a joy to behold even at that distance. She dove gracefully and swam with long strokes, a smile on her lips. I felt as if I was present at the dawn of creation when god made Eve and offered her to Adam.

She emerged from the surf a siren of the sea with flashing eyes and a beaming smile, her gorgeous curves forcing us all to recall our manners without resorting to barbarian ogling, although I admit that we ogled her. She didn't seem to mind.

We spent the day taking photographs and collecting shells. We found a large sea turtle crawling from the frothy waves and Lani marveled at its prehistoric countenance. The seas are alive with an abundance of life for those that seek it. Birds are everywhere, often traveling thousands of miles between landmasses. We saw gulls that wheeled in the air and screeched at us; and smaller birds that flit about sporadically. We captured in our nets small fish that we photographed in our endless quest to assist the world's museums in cataloging the various species. There is a debate among some that mankind has discovered all that needs discovering, and there are no mysteries in nature's abundance. To this point I disagree, for the mighty Pacific and its islands offer proof that providence has created creatures of wild origins as yet unseen.

Had time permitted I would have enjoyed traveling to such Paradise islands as Vaitape, Bora Bora and the Society Islands, but a growing sense of excitement tainted all of our actions as *The Reaper's Scythe* made headway later that afternoon, her sails billowing with exuberance. We saved fuel whenever possible and encouraged the ship to sail freely as all ships should. There is no greater feeling for a sailor than to be standing on a deck that embraces the rolling Pacific in good weather, the snap of the sails a sign of good fortune. These are waters filled mystery and beauty. Occasionally, Lani would inquire of a passing land mass, and our conversations often turned to tales of swashbucklers and pirates who may have buried their glimmering trunks of coins and jewels on any of these small outcroppings, the treasure lost forever by the passage of time.

Eight days out from Singapore and we visited but two nameless islands. At the second island—nothing more than a series of atolls clumped together on a reef—we encountered a snake in the brush that took us by surprise. Lani, standing up on the white sand, was photographing the palm trees as a reference photo for the specimens we collected from the surf, and called out when she saw the snake.

It was a python. A most unusual sight in such an isolated location. There was no other sign of life crawling on the sand or in the brush. This led us to believe the snake had survived a capsized trawler or fishing boat and somehow had survived to inhabit this small island. The python was at least six feet long. Undoubtedly; it would perish without food. I was bothered by it, although as I mentioned, encountering snakes in such faraway locations was not as implausible as it might appear.

This snake had odd markings. Its head was white. The body had yellow and white stripes punctuated by daubs of green. Doc Caspian speculated it was an albino snake, or at least partially albino. We had never seen anything like it. I wanted to capture the snake and examine it later, but when I suggested this Badoo put his hand on my arm and said in a low voice, "No, captain. This is a bad omen."

"Aye, captain," Rocco added, "let's leave the damn thing here. It makes my skin crawl. I wouldn't be able to sleep with that thing on board, even if we killed it."

So we left the snake coiled about a palm branch, its forked tongue darting in and out as its soulless eyes appraised us. Badoo may have been correct and the snake was a bad omen, for in the days to come we would encounter far too many such omens and our mettle would be tested time and again.

FOUR

For a brief time, we enjoyed a world of intense beauty and the blessings of good shipmates. The nights were breathtaking. The heavens offered us a map of stars that led to worlds yet explored, the cosmos gliding above us with such splendor that I could wish for nothing more but to stand amidships with Lani at my side and enjoy Heaven's visual bounty. Here, far from the gas lamps and choking stench of cities, we had all of these sights to ourselves, or so we thought. Even the spectral moon sometimes appeared like a pearl glimmering in a lavender display.

Lani delighted in the dolphins we saw that sometimes followed us. They leaped and chattered in a playful manner to the point where the often-somber Badoo even smiled. All thoughts of bad omens had vanished.

The ever-charming Edgar Bumpassé attempted to fatten us with his flapjacks, and nearly succeeded. Johnny Turner and Dusty Smith maintained the ship with Rocco, all of them enjoying Lani's soft presence and startling beauty, but to their credit they all abstained from the usual coarse comments such lusty men are prone to under other conditions. In fact, I privately complimented them on their gentlemanly demeanors. Having a woman aboard *The Reaper's Scythe* was a rare thing. Even the doomed Victoria Ransom had only been granted that privilege a few times.

We established an idyllic routine. Doc Caspian inquired to our health, which elicited nothing more than complaints of having devoured too many flapjacks, maple syrup and fruit. Then, of course, there were Edgar's elaborate chicken and potato dinners.

Lani took hundreds of photos. Thanks to her, I began to view the sea's many moods from a different perspective. There were mornings where the waters were cloaked in fog and the wind had vanished. Out of this stygian mist we often heard sounds that we could not explain. Once very early in the morning, as I stood with Lani on the foredeck, we distinctively heard voices speaking in English but laced with a heavy French accent. There was no explanation for it. When the sun burned the fog away there were no ships visible, nor did we encounter any other vessels during our trip to Sumtoa.

I suppose I might qualify that statement somewhat. We encountered a ship's graveyard; a stranded assortment of derelict vessels numbering about a dozen. These ships were surrounded by a thick tangle of seaweed that smelled worse than Singapore. It was quite foggy that morning and the broken masts and mildewed bows rose up from the fog like spectral warships; but upon closer inspection, we saw these were naught but ancient vessels that had remained afloat solely at the behest of that seaweed. I had seen such graveyards before, although it was a rare sight. These ships, deserted for decades (possibly longer) traveled the oceans at the tide's whim. Occasionally, such collections vanished during storms, lost beneath the waves, only to be regurgitated and set afloat again at some far distant corner of the endless sea.

The seas carry sounds, perhaps even ancient voices, set loose on a wandering breeze; and so too its waters cradle ships lost in storms or abandoned by their crew, and these things come back to us as reminders of some mariner's lost past.

The wind is another presence, as palatable as any human; as kind as a good woman or as wicked as Satan's spawn. Touched by an unseen hand, the wind brings scents of spices and meals cooking over a fire; or sometimes the fresh scent of land saturated by rain or warmed by a tropical sun. The scents and fragrances on the breeze are as varied as the rolling waves themselves.

Lani commented that a painter's greatest challenge lies in rendering a faithful adaptation of the ocean's waters. It is the rare breed of painters who can manage the task properly, and those that do capture but a solitary moment of the sea's ever-changing features.

Blazing sunsets never ceased to thrill us and they are etched in our memories forever. I recall with clarity watching the sun boil at the orange and yellow horizon while the sky above was washed in turquoise and purple. Lani's raven hair was tinged by the colors of the setting sun, her smooth brown skin an enticement that no poet, photographer or painter could ever do justice.

The days passed, and as we cut a path across the rolling seas, we experienced a growing sense of excitement. My knowledge of Sumtoa and its volcano was minimal so I enhanced my knowledge by studying my nautical charts. When we realized the sky was again full of gulls we knew land was fast approaching.

Sumtoa rose from the mist the following morning, and I felt a sense of dread as I watched its volcanic peak emerge from the sepulchral fog. Rising nearly three thousand feet, Sumtoa's volcano gave off a thin tendril of dark smoke. As we grew closer, I saw palm trees and steep hills, wild underbrush and dark crevices. Sumtoa was approximately forty-five miles in depth and circumference, and hardly ideal for human habitation. Sumtoa is encircled by a coral barrier reef teeming with aquatic life. The only access to Sumtoa's solitary beach is through a break in the reef at high tide.

The reef was visible as the sun began to lighten the island's white sandy beach. *The Reaper's Scythe* would be in harm's way by entering the encircled beach because of the narrow passage, and once inside we could not depart except on the rising tide. Initially, these facts were obvious to us but didn't bother me all that much. Still, I was cautious and instructed

Rocco to take us around the entire island first. I wanted to look around.

There were several smaller islets scattered around Sumtoa, but these were small. A man could easily walk across any of them in an hour or so. Sumtoa itself seemed like a combination of Bora-Bora and Krakatoa, both of which existed as the remnants of a volcanic eruption thousands of years ago. The volcano on Krakatoa, I recalled, exploded in 1883, sending thirty foot tsunamis at the coasts of Java and Sumatra and drowning scores of people. In short, Sumtoa was formidable.

On the island's far side, we spied through our binoculars a small pier slanted off the rocks. Although there were no signs of life, not to mention the absence of ships, it was clear the pier was of recent origin. A pier at that location could only be used for a longboat or canoe. No ship even half the size of *The Reaper's Scythe* would dare move in that close to the perilous shoreline.

Keeping in mind that the pier had a purpose, we continued around the island. The dark, volcanic rock, when visible, added a sense of gloom to the impenetrable jungle. This was an unfriendly place, almost menacing, and certainly mysterious.

Sumtoa lies closer to the Polynesian islands. As I gazed upon the rough trees and swaying palms I had no doubt that any stories about red diamonds or any precious stones being found here were entirely false. Lani's story was impossible to believe. I chanced a glance at her to see if her features showed any sign of emotion, but to her credit, she was impassive. At some point, I realized, I would have to be blunt and explain that this voyage was most likely a fool's errand.

Coming around again to the reef, I studied the azure water inside the circle of coral. The blue water varied in shade. The shades were round very much like a bulls-eye, with the dark purple oval an indication the depth dropped to a dangerous level in the circle's center. Outside of that oval the water was light blue and shallow near the beach. This was a most unusual geographic formation, and I surmised it might have been caused by the very volcanic eruption that formed the island.

After a brief discussion, I decided we would pass the reef at high tide and anchor, and then set out for a brief exploration the following day. Since two high tides and two low tides occur every lunar day, or approximately twice in twenty-four hours, we had only to wait for high tide.

"Do you have any idea where your father might be found on this island," I asked Lani as she studied the island through my binoculars.

"No, but he's here," she said hopefully, "I can sense it."

"And what about these natives? I find it hard to believe that this island is home to any but the wild beast."

"He's here all the same," Lani responded, "and the sooner we find my father the better off we'll all be."

Entering the surrounding reef was an easier action than we had anticipated. It was already late afternoon, and all of us stood on deck and studied the azure water. The sudden drop in depth that I mentioned was unusual and slightly unnerving. All around us were the softer tones of a light blue sky, but at its center the water darkened as the reef gave way, plunging to an unknown depth. That dark patch of water about two hundred yards from shore was less than fifty yards in circumference, and more than a little ominous.

Doc Caspian surmised the reef must be perched on an undersea cliff and the dark section was the place where the outcropping had sheared off during a volcanic eruption. It was possible that the ocean's bottom was over a thousand feet below us, and accessible here only by diving straight down. This was not a prospect that any of us would entertain.

At sunset, the sky was awash in fiery red and molten yellow hues that took our breaths away. Even Edgar emerged from his kitchen and sat with us awhile on deck to marvel at the sunset and study the mysterious island. Johnny, Dusty and Badoo ventured to swim for a while before joining us on deck. They reported the water was warm, as expected, and the reef was alive with colorful fish. There was no sign of sharks; possibly due to the fact the reef was isolated. We all watched a large turtle swim ashore and crawl along the beach. There were plenty of seagulls nearby. A few of them took a perch high on our mainsail's crossbeam.

Lani, Rocco, Badoo and I spent most of our time making small talk and keeping an eye on the island. Perhaps we all sensed a change in the air; or each of us had a premonition that we could not explain.

Just before dark, we heard the drumbeats. They were neither loud nor distinctive. They were simply faint drumbeats. I could not ascertain their location, but it was obvious they originated from deep in the island's jungle, and perhaps at a higher elevation. I strained my eyes scrutinizing the gloom for a sign of a campfire, but there was nothing.

I know that Lani was thrilled. The drumbeats proved that the island was occupied. Badoo chose that moment to remind me of an unfortunate fact of which I was already aware.

"Captain, being anchored inside a reef puts us at a tactical disadvantage should we be attacked before high tide."

"We have plenty of guns and ammunition." I countered.

"We are facing unknown adversaries."

"I have cartridges for the Thompson." I reminded him.

Badoo nodded. He'd said his piece and appeared satisfied. And I had to admit he had a point. Of course, we had ample firepower. The Thompson sub-machine gun wasn't only a favorite of Chicago gangsters. We had two on board and several thousand rounds of ammunition. Rocco would carry one and so would I. We all had our .45 automatics. Dusty had a Winchester rifle, and we had a Mauser on board and several other handguns.

I gave the order that all of us, including Edgar and Doc, would carry a gun at all times. My crew never questioned such an order. They would even sleep with their guns. We had been through some close shaves together and none of us took foolish chances.

The drumbeats lasted about an hour. Then an eerie silence descended on the island. We were about to turn in when something disturbed the water off the stern. Something big. We all heard a splash and when we went to look, all we saw in the lantern light were rippling waves.

Obviously, a large creature, perhaps a dolphin, had broken the surface. I realize now that I never accepted that hypothesis. Most of us had been at sea so long and witnessed so many of the sea's marvels that we knew strange and mysterious things were commonplace out here among the faraway islands. Nature followed its own set of rules, and sometimes science was at a loss to explain it.

A quarter moon cast a silvery sheen over the rippling cove. I encouraged Lani to turn in but she declined. In fact, even Doc and Edgar, being the oldest and usually the first to turn in, remained on deck.

Interesting tidbits come back to me after all of these weeks. Initially, we had wooden folding deck chairs with canvas seats set-up so that we might relax, but as the sun went down we all remained standing. I was not conscious of this fact at the time. We all must have sensed the danger without realizing it.

The Reaper's Scythe rocked suddenly as struck by a turbulent sea. I heard the splashing in the same instant I saw a tendril whip across the deck. The legendary Kraken, a creature that too many educated men insist is but a creature of mythology.

My first impression was of the tendril that snaked across the deck. The skin was a dark gray but mottled as if by a disease with patches of white and lighter shades of gray. The effect reminded me of a paint-splattered limb.

"We are facing unknown adversaries."

I barked for Lani to dash below to safety while Badoo shouted an alarm. I saw Badoo sprinting for his harpoon that hung on the wall near the cabin door. Lani, being too startled to argue, did as she was told. Once I saw her safely descend to the quarters, I had my .45 in hand, although I abstained from firing.

It will appear contradictory that I would hesitate in firing upon the Kraken, especially after my description of the gun battle in Singapore where I took human life when rescuing Lani. I have no defense. I contain multitudes, as Walt Whitman once said.

The scientist in me was fascinated by the size of the creature. This was no common specimen of *Octopus vulgaris*, and I wanted to study it. However, our immediate problem being the fact that it had attached itself to the stern and its weight put us in danger of being capsized. Additionally, its eight arms bearing two rows of suckers each, were controlled by a rather advanced brain. An octopus is, no matter my scientific interest, a carnivorous marine mollusk, and this one was undoubtedly hungry. Those tendrils were looking for food.

The ship rocked back and forth, and rushing forward I had a glimpse in the pale moonglow of the creature's two soulless, dark eyes appraising me.

A tendril whipped at my head and I dodged, slipping on the deck. I landed unceremoniously on my back, the .45 still held tightly in my hand.

I heard Badoo utter a wild scream, but I knew this to be his warrior's yell. He plunged the harpoon at the tendril and withdrew it. The razored harpoon barely had an effect. Rocco pulled me to my feet, a string of wild curses flinging from his lips.

Two additional tendrils came lashing toward us, dripping seaweed and smelling like a pungent mold. I saw the Kraken staring at us as he strengthened his hold on the ship. Its size was tremendous. The tendril's purpose was to lure its victims close so that the Kraken could strike with its beak and inject its victim with a paralyzing poison.

Badoo struck again with his harpoon just as Dusty and Johnny called for us to stay low. Shots rang out as they fired wildly at the animal. A few slugs struck the tendrils, which only slowed the creature nominally.

Lurching to my knees, I aimed my gun at one of its eyes and a chill swept through me. Even an average octopus has the most well developed eye in the invertebrate world, and it was obvious this creature was watching me. It was unnerving. I fired once and I'm embarrassed to report for once my hand must have been shaking. My shot went astray.

A deadly pantomime ensued.

In the moonglow, faint though it was, I saw the tendrils wriggle up and over the deck. Those enormous rows of suckers meant certain doom for any of us coming in contact with them.

Just as quickly the silence was broken as my crew took up their guns again.

As if in slow motion, I became conscious of Doc and Edgar firing their automatics; and simultaneously Johnny let loose with a blistering round from his Winchester. The roar of the guns and the tinkle of brass against the deck was deafening.

All the while, the tendrils never ceased their motion.

Curling and slapping at the ship, they sought sustenance and each of us were scrambling to stay out of their deadly grasp.

I was dumbfounded by the lack of effect our guns were having. I saw that the creature's tendrils were gore-splattered, but even wounded it was on a relentless quest. I had never seen anything like it.

Dusty was knocked aside, and for a breathless moment I thought he would become entangled by a tendril, but he crawled out of reach. Rocco had emptied his .45 and cursed fluently as he ejected the clip, retrieved a fresh clip from his belt, and slapped it into place.

I could still feel that horrid but somehow majestic creature's eyes on me. Then in one blinding instant I realized the only course of action that might save us.

Lurching toward the harpoon rack, I was reminded that this rack had been installed at Badoo's insistence. Although Badoo was proficient in the use of modern firearms, he was trained at sea by men he once said were, "The more ancient of the mariners, trained themselves in a lost past, relics themselves of a bygone age." All sailing ships must inevitably carry a few harpoons.

I grabbed one from the rack and joined Badoo near the railing. We were of the same mind, each of us knowing what must be done. Badoo had sweat dripping from his brow, and his white teeth gleamed when he smiled at me.

"Captain, you're not as well versed in the use of a harpoon as I am."

"We have to plunge it into its brain. It's the only way to stop it."

Before I could say another word, Badoo had yanked the harpoon free of my hand and roughly shoved me aside. Then, with a harpoon in each hand, he dashed toward a sliding tendril, which quickly wrapped itself about his body. I was struck mute by the scene.

Badoo was lifted, still grinning. We watched in horror as the Kraken swiftly dropped into the water with Badoo a victim of its wriggling tentacle, his war cry echoing in the gloom as he disappeared below the surface.

None of us spoke. A minute ticked past with agonizing slowness. The ship settled itself on the rocking swells as if nothing had occurred. The abrupt silence was unnerving. Another minute ticked past. We watched the water but all we saw were fragments of the moon shattered across the dark waves.

Eventually, a short string of bubbles broke the surface. Then more bubbles, and a moment later Badoo splashed to the surface. He carried but one harpoon. I tossed him a rope and we hauled him aboard.

"It took a bit of doing," was all he said, "but it's done."

"How far down did it drag you?" I asked.

"It's deep here, too deep...maybe fifty feet before I harpooned it."

"All right," I slapped him on the shoulder. Badoo was one of the most fearless men I have ever sailed with. "Are you certain it's dead?"

"No, of course not." He said flatly, "but it's injured severely. Let's hope it finds food elsewhere."

Doc, Rocco, Edgar, Dusty and Johnny had gathered near us. Johnny said, "The octopus may have been curious. Its endless search for food and this ship's proximity was an encouragement in its quest to eat."

We discussed our options. Doc was in favor of moving out of the inlet, but I wasn't keen on anchoring in the open sea near reefs. Eventually, I decided to move into shallower water with the idea this might discourage another visit. Still, our options were limited. The low tide was dangerous and *The Reaper's Scythe* was a heavy ship. Getting lodged onto a sandbar could prove our undoing. When Lani came up from below deck, I took one look at her and decided to risk it anyway. We were committed to looking for her father.

Badoo was enthusiastic about his encounter with the giant octopus. We celebrated his survival with a small snort of bourbon each. Dusty and Johnny volunteered to stay up all night watching for a return visit from the slimy monster. I knew they'd be exhausted come morning, but they were young and enjoyed the danger.

I thought Lani was nervous. This was the first sign of trepidation I had seen in her, and I wondered if the Kraken had unnerved her.

"Badoo injured the brute," I assured her. "I think we'll be safe for a little while."

"It's not that," she said. "I was thinking of my father. Now that we're here, I can see how wild this place really is. Do you think there's any chance that he's alive?"

"If he is we'll find him," I promised. I placed my hand on her shoulder, but she moved away. It was obvious she wanted to be alone.

"We'll get an early start," I said, but she had turned her back to me to stand at the rail and study the shoreline. I left her alone.

Sleep was difficult that night. Too much had happened in a short period for me to relax. Shortly after midnight, I rose from my bunk and went up to visit with Dusty and Johnny. I shouldn't have been surprised to find Rocco and Badoo with them. They were smoking and talking quietly amongst themselves like conspirators. Therefore, while Doc, Edgar and Lani counted sheep, we made plans for the expedition. The island rose up from the sea like the silhouette of a giant outlined against a starry tableau. I couldn't see the jungle in the dark as I looked at the shoreline, but I could sense it, and I didn't like the feeling at all.

FIVE

Badoo stayed aboard *The Reaper's Scythe* with Doc and Edgar. He had the Thompson sub-machine gun and enough guts to handle anything. If the Kraken made an appearance, I had no doubt that Badoo would make the creature regret any further deck-side exploration.

Dusty and Johnny and Rocco were armed, too. This time I let Rocco carry the other Thompson. I carried some food supplies and sleeping bags in a backpack. My own sidearm was the 1911 Colt. Dusty also carried a backpack with supplies.

Lani was dressed in khaki. She had borrowed a safari hat with a leopard skin band, which gave her a rather fanciful look; like one of these characters in the pulp magazines. We took the longboat ashore and all the while she stared at the palm trees and rolling hills beyond. The dawn had broken warm and bright and I knew how hot it would get in a very short period of time.

Once ashore, we pulled the boat up so that it wouldn't be touched by the high tide, and then we explored the beach. Other than some small animal tracks in the sand, there was no sign of life. We remained within view of Badoo who watched from the deck.

We began looking for trails into the jungle. This took some time. It was obvious this was an untouched beach; known only to gulls and small lizards that scampered about. Eventually, we found a thin strand of scrub-brush that might have been an animal trail at one time. I signaled to Badoo that we would enter the jungle. He waved. Having decided to remain ashore until we determined one way or another if professor Joseph Kawena was alive, or if he was on the island at all, it was time we began to search in earnest. Yet I had my doubts about everything.

Once we broke through the trees, we found ourselves beneath an immense jungle canopy. Suddenly the sunlight was filtered through vines and elephant palms. The breeze was blocked and the humidity rose considerably.

Almost immediately, we were greeted by the chattering of angry, small monkeys. They swung around above us, disturbed by our sudden appearance, and they let us know that we were not welcome. One of them actually threw something at us; a twig or small coconut. The sound they made was tremendous. We had seen such things before on islands across the Pacific, but never in such an oddly wild and haunted place as the Sumtoa jungle.

Our familiarity with jungles aided us in our trek across Sumtoa. Our encounters with wildlife were unsurprising albeit still thrilling. The many colorful birds and snakes that we passed all added another level of excitement to our exploration. There were also small rodents and myriad insects. Once we encountered a large web strung between trees. The spider clinging to it was a ferocious and lethal looking thing of eight inches diameter with yellow markings. My first instinct was to kill it, but instead I asked Lani to photograph it. It wouldn't do for a scientific expedition to randomly kill any life forms it encountered.

Life under the jungle canopy is a world unto itself. Rocco and I had learned long ago that a night spent in the jungle was fraught with peril. Once in the Peruvian jungle we were besieged by thousands of clattering insects that emerged from the underbrush in great waves. Many of these were black beetles half the size of a man's fist, fast and persistent. I had encountered fire ants and strange little blue and green winged creatures and moths that emitted a foul scent. There was no end to the variety of insects that roam this fair earth, many of which have yet to be photographed and categorized. If time had permitted we might have done a better job of documenting the colorful life forms that we witnessed, but our immediate goal on behalf of Lani was to locate her father.

There were two moments in that dense jungle worth mentioning. The first involves our discovery that Sumtoa was home to several Komodo dragons. This surprised us. The Komodo dragons were a relatively new species in the scientific community; having been discovered some twenty years earlier on the islands of Komodo, Rinea, Flores and Gili Montag. We had traveled to those islands a year earlier to photograph them for the Natural History Museum. *Varanus komodoensis* was a lizard weighing on average 150 lbs, sometimes exceeding ten feet long. Komodo dragons are extremely dangerous carnivores and have been known to attack humans. Their scaled greenish-brown skin is tough but a .45 at close range could penetrate it. They live primarily on small game, and we had no intentions of getting close to them. We encountered them at the jungle periphery, just before breaking through into a clearing of grassland that lay low in a valley bordering the volcanic hills.

These Komodo dragons put us on alert. We spied four of them lumbering about in the grasslands. Their presence confirmed a supply of small game was present to sustain their existence, but we weren't certain how large a population might thrive on Sumtoa. I suspected less than a dozen could survive here. One was dangerous enough. As a result of this, we were forced to circle the grassland rather than cutting across in a straight line. This added several hours to our morning trek.

Shortly, we made a second discovery that would later shed light on the many mysteries of Sumtoa Island. At the jungle's edge on the northwestern side we found a crumbling wooden shack that might have been a sanctuary for some lost Christian missionary. There was an old Bible inside, moldy and brittle to the touch, and a foot-long golden crucifix. The gold was tarnished and the crucifix was badly battered. It was hardly beautiful, but gold is beautiful because of its monetary value and not for aesthetics. The base had been broken and was missing.

The shack was furnished with a crude wood table, two chairs and various clay pots and cups. The remnants of a cloth blanket were visible in one corner. Outside we found what I believe was a grave. It was no more than a mound of mossy earth, but it was in a section where the forest bed was flat and the incongruous hump was too similar to a six-foot long grave.

We kept the crucifix. I had Dusty store it in his backpack. We were about to turn away when Johnny spotted some clay tablets half-hidden by clumps of leaves and part of the broken wall. The tablets all had Chinese etchings. We recognized the Chinese characters although none of us could read them. We saved three tablets, the three that were salvageable as some of the others were broken beyond repair.

The strange Chinese tablets, the moldering Bible and the grave all lent us to speculating on the origins of this old dwelling. Here was evidence of different cultures, so far removed from each other that it seemed impossible to encounter them in such a remote location.

With these artifacts stored in Dusty's backpack, he complained of the added weight and I promised him a slug of bourbon when we finally made camp that night. I wanted to get into the hills opposite the grasslands where an encounter with the Komodo dragons was less likely. The Komodo dragons preferred the lowlands and through my binoculars, I saw a series of rolling hills and switchbacks that looked promising.

We had traveled further west than I intended because of the Komodo dragons and when we cut north, again we had a clear view of the ocean when we crested the first hill. Something caught my eye on the undulating horizon. When I looked through the lenses, I saw a freighter in the distance. It was still too far away to make out any details, but it wasn't big. I estimated it was a small cargo ship. What was interesting was the fact it was coming straight toward Sumtoa Island. If the freighter were visiting Bora Bora, it would already have turned south. If my hunch was right, we were going to have visitors.

Since that day, I have wondered why I wasn't surprised. The simple fact is that anything involving Victoria Ransom would include any number of surprises. No, I wasn't surprised. If anything, I was eager to locate Professor Joseph Kawena and put to rest this absurd notion that Sumtoa Island was home to a cache of red diamonds.

Once into the hills the threat from the dragons was diminished. The rolling hills before us undoubtedly split into several other valleys that lie in the shadow of the great volcano. We had noticed an occasional string of smoke from the volcano's top, but as yet there was no sign of serious activity. A scan of the area with binoculars failed to reveal any lava flows.

It was the next hill that revealed the first sign of human habitation. Nestled on a far hillside I could just see a row of beige buildings. They were partially hidden by the palms and flowering brush. Sumtoa Island was equally as colorful as any island we'd visited, and it took time for the eyes to adjust to the ever-changing colors. Each bend in the trail, or the top of each hill brought forth a dazzling display of nature's beauty as the sun began its slow slide toward the horizon.

Late in the afternoon on that first day, I became aware of another presence. At first I thought it was some wild animal, perhaps some species of cat like a leopard, but I took no extra precautions. As the day wore on, I had flashes of it in the greenery. It moved like a man. Dusty was the first to say something.

"Forty feet up to our left," he said, moving next to me. "I just saw something. Might be a native, maybe a big fellow."

"I saw it too."

Rocco's expression told me he was aware of our visitor it as well. He looked at Johnny and so through a silent communication everything was changed. Lani, at the time, was unaware of this. She appeared intent on making time and getting up into the hills where she hoped to find her father. I sensed she was determined not to show any sign of fatigue, and I thought it was to her credit that she showed us such resolve. She was, and remains, a remarkably strong woman.

We decided to camp in the foothills, and we chose our spot carefully. It was Rocco who found the clearing where we cut a lean-to from the foliage and made a place for Lani to sleep. Johnny carved out a circle in the earth and made a fire with deadfall. There were plenty of dried branches. Dusty and Rocco set to cooking some soup that Edgar had prepared. We heated the soup over the fire as the molten sun began to sink at the end of the world, or so it appeared to us. From this vantage point, we could look out over the marshland where we'd encountered the Komodo dragons and see the glittering waves catch the last rays of the dying sunlight. It was a beautiful sight and under different circumstances, I might have enjoyed it sitting next to Lani as I was.

Lani had spoken little during the day. She was pensive, but pleasant when we spoke. I assured her that we had made good time, and that tomorrow we should reach those dwellings I had seen through the binoculars.

"I know," she said, "it's just that I was hoping to meet the natives right away. I wasn't prepared for the immensity of this place."

"It is quite an imposing piece of rock, and the jungle and these hills are very dense. All the same, another day's journey and we'll be up near those huts or whatever they are."

"And you're sure you didn't see any sign of life?"

"No, nothing."

"He must be alive," she said.

"If he is we'll find him," I promised. "I want you to eat something and get some rest. We've a long day tomorrow."

She laughed then, and I thought I might have sounded too paternal. "Of course." Was all she said, and then she ate the soup. Not long after, she curled up in the blankets we'd given her and went to sleep under the lean-to.

Johnny and Dusty were eager to explore the area but I advised caution.

"We don't know enough about the natives here, and I don't want to inadvertently alarm them. You can circumnavigate a reasonable perimeter and let's wait to see if anyone comes close during the night."

"Whoever it is he was on our trail from the moment we entered the foothills," Rocco said, "and he's big. Very big."

Dusty and Johnny split up, each circling the camp before meeting again. They saw nothing, heard nothing. Being younger men, they were more prone to embrace action and I saw the disappointment in their faces.

We had brewed some coffee and later I let the fire die down. We didn't want to make ourselves easy targets, but we also had no intention of hiding. Rocco and I stayed closer to Lani who had fallen into a deep sleep. Johnny and Dusty took up positions in the dark perimeter. I realize now that we all had the feeling that something was going to happen. We were, in fact, expecting a visitor.

There passed an interminable stretch of blackness mingled with the soft crackling of the fire and the lingering scent of the night's sea-breeze that reminded us of the great distance we had traveled across water.

Dusty had the first inkling of our visitor. He motioned to us with a quick signal of his palm, his thumb cocked off toward the woods. It must have been close to midnight, or just after. I heard nothing. None of us made any obvious movement. I was confident, as we all were that we could brandish our weapons with ease and repel any obvious attack. Of course, we didn't know yet if our visitor was curious or meant us harm. My immediate hope being that this was our first contact with the natives of Sumtoa, and from them we might learn of Professor Joseph Kawena's fate.

Rocco and I were sitting on logs near the dwindling fire. Johnny was behind us. Dusty was directly across from me so I could see everything that happened. Rocco had turned slightly, his head angled toward Dusty. I had glanced at Rocco whose eyes were fixed on the darkness beyond Dusty. There was a flicker of amazement in his features as I suddenly realized our visitor had arrived.

I turned my gaze back in time to see an enormous brute propel himself from the darkness brandishing a club. An arm corded with thick sinews swung the club so swiftly that it was a blur. Dusty's arm was shattered with a sickening crack, his Winchester rifle knocked from his hands. In the dim light of our fading campfire, I saw the creature and felt a sinking, cold sensation. It was a man, but not a normal man at all. Standing over six and a half feet tall, his ridged brow was rather like a Mongolian, but far more prominent. His teeth were brown with decay, his nose flattened as if it had been severely broken and never repaired. Malice shone clearly in the black eyes that swept an evil gaze over us. The man—the creature—had no hair. He wore tattered and baggy cotton trousers cut-off just below the knees and tied with a rope. The chest, arms and thighs were enormous, the muscles rippling with thick veins that undulated like living things just below the surface of his flesh. The ears were pointed; deformed possibly at birth like the rest of him.

Later, I would think it was all a trick of the light and shadows on that distant jungle hill, but I know he was all too real.

Rocco fired and missed only because of the creature's speed. Lifting its head, he bellowed. Such a horrifying sound I have never heard since. It was at once a scream of anguish and rage.

Then he was gone. I had not taken a breath. So stunned was I that I had only managed to bring up the .45 automatic and point it feebly by the time this had all occurred. Rocco had fired one shot. Dusty lay moaning on the ground. Johnny came over and fired three times into the darkness. Lani, roused from her sleep, stared in uncomprehending horror at all of us.

SIX

The torturous night was alive with sounds that suddenly were ominous at every turn. The common crackle of leaves or of small animals foraging for food now telegraphed a potential attack by the giant beast-man. I do not know what to call him. He was a beast-man, and as I pen these words all of these weeks later I am reminded of *The Island of Dr. Moreau* by H. G. Wells, which I had read during my impressionable youth. Sumtoa had become such a place of terror, and while I harbored no thought that a mad scientist had created the beast-man, I was nonetheless aware that such fanciful tales no longer seemed far-fetched. The sea had brought us here and so filled with mystery is the sea, that I will never again question a sailor's tale of mighty serpents or the dangerous monsters of long forgotten lands.

Dusty's arm appeared fractured, but fortunately the bone had not splintered and broken through the skin. No doubt Doc Caspian might chastise us for the crude splint and sling we made for him, but it was the best we could do. Dusty, to his credit, immediately began practicing holding and aiming his rifle with one arm in a sling.

My intention was to turn back to the ship at first light. Dusty's safety and Lani's safety was now paramount. Lani was crestfallen but claimed that she understood that Dusty might do with some medical attention. I also didn't like that the beast-man had attacked so quickly. His speed and size made him a formidable opponent, especially in the dark. The beast-man knew every nook and cranny of the island and we didn't.

We discovered at first light that returning to the ship wouldn't be quite that easy. After breaking camp, we had gone downhill sixty or so yards when we encountered the beast-man again, and he wasn't alone.

"There are dozens of them, captain." Rocco said as his .45 appeared in his hand.

"I can pick a few off from here." Dusty said, manipulating his rifle into his injured hand. "I owe that big bruiser something."

We recognized the beast-man from the night before, and with him down the trail were indeed a dozen others. Several of the men were slightly smaller, but not by much. Each had similar features, including the sagittal hump above the eyes and the flat nose, which we surmised, was an inbred genetic defect. Could they be a lost race of Cro-Magnon types, unknown to the world until now?

A few of them wore sandals and crude shirts made from animal skins. All of them brandished clubs or spears, and none of them took their hate-filled eyes from us. We were not welcome here, and they clearly meant us harm.

"Look how they're keeping back," Johnny pointed out. "It's almost as if they understand that we have powerful weapons."

Johnny raised his .45 and fired once into the air. At the sound of the thundering gun, the beast-men fell back a little more, but bellowed angrily in their guttural language.

With the Thompson sub-machinegun, I might easily mow them down, but taking lives unnecessarily wasn't part of my moral beliefs. I couldn't do it, and my crew knew this from experience. I wasn't afraid to kill, but I only did so in extreme circumstances and when there was no other solution, as there hadn't been in Singapore when we rescued Lani. These beast-men lived here, and we were intruders.

"The trail is too narrow and there's no way around them." Rocco said.

I turned and looked up into the hills where the beige buildings were barely visible through the green fronds and palms. Had I just glimpsed movement up near the largest building?

"We're going up." I announced. "And keep in mind we still have to come down. All we're doing is delaying the inevitable. We'll have to get past them somehow."

There were no protests. If anything, they were relieved to get on with achieving our goal. Lani looked nervous but her determination shone through. She was not surprisingly the first to turn up the trail and begin the hardest part of our trek. The hills were steep and we had to master several precarious switchbacks and rocky formations occluded by scrub before reaching the village.

The beast-men followed us. They made no effort to conceal themselves. The only thing they did, as a form of protection was to keep a safe distance back. I had the Thompson sub-machine gun, and for the first time in my life, I didn't want to use it.

"Captain, they're just dumb brutes. I don't think they know any better."

"You're right, Rocco, but that won't stop them from killing us if the opportunity presents itself."

The beast-men were familiar with the terrain and several of them had slipped alongside us. They peered at us from behind rocks or trees, the malevolence plainly showing on their faces. Once, one of them leaned out and swung his club at Dusty who ducked just in time. If it had landed, the blow might have killed him. Dusty discharged his gun harmlessly into the brush, which sent the beast scrambling away.

They were edging closer and willing to take more chances. This is where I paused as the sun bathed us in a hot molten glow, the wild fecund scent of the jungle nearly overwhelming us. There was no wind suddenly and very little sound. I had to keep the beast-men away but I didn't want to kill any of them. I realized they wouldn't give me a choice.

The Thompson sub-machine gun is possibly the most destructive of all firearms that a man can carry in his own hands. The one in my hands was a twin of the one Badoo had aboard *The Reaper's Scythe*, a model M1921 with a 100 round drum and capable of automatic fire that pushes 820 rounds per minute. This means my 100 rounds would expel in seconds. In Chicago they call it "The Organ Grinder" or "The Chicago Typewriter." I paid $200.00 each for our "Tommy Guns."

The Thompson is heavy and firing it accurately doesn't involve marksmanship. The rounds from a Thompson blow out so fast that they destroy anything they hit. One sweep and you can fell half a dozen men, probably more. Once the trigger is engaged, the barrel erupts with a streak of flame as the rounds explode into the air. This is a fearsome and formidable killing machine.

"Captain, they're just dumb brutes."

I lifted the Thompson and pressed the trigger and sent a spray of flaming lead into the jungle above their heads. The beast-men screamed in terror and retreated. We watched them loping into the brush and shouting angrily. None of them looked back at us. They melted into the jungle.

Rather than press our luck, I ordered everyone to move up the trail. That was the last we would see of the beast-men for a few days. Rocco, being infinitely wise and prone to blunt statements, pointed out thirty minutes later that going home meant avoiding contact with both the beast-men *and* the Komodo dragons. Rather than worry about it, we moved higher into the hills.

We were surprised to discover the trail was difficult to climb. The ancient lava flows had built hills along the ridge that were often impossible to climb. This, combined with the jungle's thickness slowed our progress dramatically. Combined with the heat, we began to suffer from exhaustion. Our clothing was soaked with sweat, our breathing labored.

Not long after we discovered a small hidden valley. It dipped between an ancient lava flow on one side and thick brush on the other. I surveyed the area carefully through the binoculars to make certain there weren't any new surprises. There were palm trees in the valley and a small pond. I assumed this was a rainwater basin. We hiked down to the pond and a quick taste confirmed my suspicions. Still, we wouldn't drink the water in quantity without boiling it. We had plenty of water in our canteens and rainstorms were common enough if we needed refills.

The trail past the rainwater pond led directly up into the hillside village we had spotted earlier. We began yet another trek upwards. Rocco, being ever vigilante, was the first one to notice that we were being followed again, but not by the beast-men.

"Captain, there's a small person off in the brush on the right. He's been following us for about ten minutes."

"A small person?"

"A little more than five feet. He's wearing some colorful garb but I didn't get a good look. He's good, very quiet, and keeps just out of sight."

"I saw him too," Johnny said, "except he's a she. It's a woman judging by the figure, but I haven't had a look at her face yet."

"Well, we all know what these island women look like," Dusty said. "Remember that tribe in New Guinea? God-awful ugly as a pack mule with scurvy."

The trail was narrow and there was a profusion of volcanic boulders that forced us to climb over them. It would be some time before I saw the woman myself as we were busy climbing the more difficult part of the trail.

"Hold on," I said. "If she's following us, then she knows a better way up and down. Let's hold up here and see what develops."

"But we're almost there," Lani pleaded. "Can't we press on a little further?"

"I know you're anxious, but we're already exhausted. It's getting late anyway and we'll need to make camp. I'm not giving up, but I have to think about everyone's safety here."

Lani was disappointed but didn't press the issue, which was to her credit. From time to time I saw her study the village on the hillside above us and once I gave her the binoculars for a better view. My original estimate to reach the village that day was obviously incorrect, and it was frustrating to be so close only to find ourselves stalled.

We set up camp and ate the bacon we fried in a pan, some biscuits and coffee. We also had some fruit we picked on the island itself; some bananas and pineapples. These actions were blatant on our part. I hoped the scent of the bacon would interest the Sumtoan native that was following us. Remarkably, there was no sign of the her. We kept our guns out of sight but within easy reach.

The sun began to smolder at the edge of the world surrounded by a pale blue sky while above us the galaxies were already visible with stars winking from a velvet universe. Lani sat on a boulder near the edge of our camp where she could see the ocean and crane her neck to watch a meteor show that suddenly streaked into view like a fireworks display. Her eyes were filled with wonder and so I sat next to her without speaking. We watched the meteors flare to their demise in the atmosphere, and we watched the way the sky changed color every few moments as the sun dipped out of view like a gold coin submerged in a turquoise bowl. I waited until I heard the campfire crackling behind us and the darkness had crept closer before gently touching her shoulder. She gazed at me for a moment and I thought she might say something, but neither one of us had yet to find the right words.

We joined the others by the fire but there was no sign of our native tracker. Rocco took the opportunity to discuss a reasonable plan of action. Our original intention would have been to send Dusty or Johnny back with a report to Badoo, Doc and Edgar, however, the burst of machinegun fire had undoubtedly tipped Badoo off that we had met some type of resistance. My crew's standing orders were to investigate cautiously at the first sign of trouble. Badoo would have done so anyway if he hadn't received word from us after three days, but the machinegun noise would spur him into action sooner.

"Ask Rocco and Johnny to flip a coin," I said, "and the winner leaves at first light. Badoo will be on the hunt. Hopefully we left enough sign for him to follow."

"He can find us in the dark," Rocco said. "That Zulu is a witch doctor. He gives me the creeps."

"He's good in a fight and fearless."

"That he is. No doubt he put a hex on the old Kraken. There's no other explanation for his survival."

Johnny lost or won the coin toss depending on your point of view. I gave him the Thompson. Rocco took possession of the backpack with our food supplies and I made certain that Johnny had an extra clip for his automatic.

Once we settled into a comfortable silence, I took the first watch. Lani had already curled up into her blanket without saying much. Nightfall was a relief from the blistering heat and the sea breeze was cooler that evening.

That was when we felt the first tremor from the volcano, which until that point had shown no sign of life. Rocco and I were the only two awake.

"This is one of the world's bad places," Rocco said. "I can feel it. We need to get off this island. If her father is alive we take him and go."

"I can't imagine if he's alive or not at this point. Initially I didn't think so, but now I'm not so sure. There are mysteries here."

"Leave the mysteries to those fellows we listen to on the radio, like The Shadow. He can have all the mysteries. Those beast-men will be back, Captain, I promise you that, and we need to be ready. I saw it in their eyes."

I nodded. Rocco was, of course, correct in what he said. Those beast-men were abominations, and while I had tried to respect their right to live here, I also knew that they wouldn't do the same for us. A confrontation was inevitable as long as we stayed on the island.

"Besides, Captain," Rocco continued. "If you can save her father, then you and that beautiful young lady will have a lot to talk about won't you? I never expected a bachelor's life for you." Rocco's laughter matched the merriment in his eyes.

"Keep it down," I said, glancing over at Lani's sleeping form. "I don't want to wake anyone up."

Rocco was intrinsically Italian in every sense; ready to fight at a moment's notice, versed in the ways of love, knowledgeable on history, and possessing an uncanny sense of people and places. His instincts had saved us many times. His vast knowledge of the world often surprised me. Rocco's statement about Sumtoa being a bad place struck a chord with me more than his feeling about any potential relationship I might nurture with Lani.

"I say we pile it on if those beast-men come at us again. I'm as friendly as the next bloke but those pointy-eared bastards aren't the type to sit down with us and discuss Socratic principals. We'll give them a good dose of lead poisoning and be done with it."

"Let's concentrate on finding her father," I said, trying to change the subject, "and we'll fight when we have to."

"That's more like it."

Rocco, apparently satisfied now that he had said his piece, took the opportunity to wipe out and clean his automatic, which didn't require any service. Rocco was itching for a fight, and we would have one soon enough. I think we both sensed it.

I didn't sleep well that night. What dreams I had washed away on the night wind and I listened to the jungle. The slight occasional rumble of the earth spoke of a future eruption. I was anxious for daylight now to see if the volcano showed any sign of smoke or ash.

At four A.M., Rocco and I picked up on rustling sounds. Dusty was awake, too, and he had his rifle propped across his sling. We roused Johnny and Lani and whispered instructions. There was no question that we were being watched; but it was still too dark to see anything.

Johnny, who was prepared to begin his trek to find Badoo, who was undoubtedly making his way towards us, had moved closer to the periphery of our camp. He was staring intently into the verdant undergrowth as the world slowly brightened.

In retrospect, it appeared as if the minutes dragged by. Johnny said something but I couldn't make it out. I heard a voice respond; a soft voice. I saw a flash of blue and a young girl stepped into the camp. We were stunned to hear her speak English, albeit with a heavy accent.

"Hello, I am Satina. You must come with me."

She smiled when she said it. Lani was on her feet and confronting the girl before Rocco and I could stop her.

"My father. Do you know my father? Professor Joseph Kawena?"

"Jo-Jo? Yes, Jo-Jo wants to speak with you. Come now. Come with me."

"Where is he? Where is my father?"

"You must come with me."

Satina wore a blue and white flower print sarong style dress that clung to her lithe figure. Her hair was dark like Lani's and her eyes were green. Her smile and her beauty had an immediate effect on Johnny who stood transfixed in front of her. His lopsided grin was like that of a kid who suddenly realized he is getting a fantastic Christmas present.

"Hold on," I ordered. "Did Professor Kawena—Jo-Jo—did he send you here?"

"Yes. You must come with me. There is danger here." She gestured down the trail that we had followed, but again she was giving us that dazzling smile. Rocco stepped away and went downhill, partially out of view. I heard him curse. A few moments later he came back and said, "Captain, those cavemen are back, and there's more of them this time. You'd better take a look."

When I looked, I saw the most fearsome sight imaginable. There were at least thirty of the beasts lined up along the trail. They were in formation, each of them holding a spear. They had painted themselves in a manner that reminded me of a Sioux warrior's facial warpaint.

"Pack up camp," I said to Rocco under my breath. "Quickly."

The beast-men began chanting. They stomped their feet and chanted, all of them looking at me. I cannot adequately describe the sound they made. It was a guttural exclamation, a proclamation of their obvious intent, and it didn't bode well for us.

I looked back at Satina.

"We must go now," she said still smiling. "It will be very good to go now."

Indeed, it would be, I thought. We abandoned our plan of having Johnny seek out Badoo. For an interminably long moment everything was suspended in time and moving in slow-motion. Dusty and Johnny gathering our belongings, Rocco coming up next to me with his .45 in hand, and the sight of Lani following Satina into the jungle to follow some undiscovered path that presumably led us to safety.

The beast-men charged.

Rocco let loose with two quick shots but they were still too far away for any hope that a handgun might do them harm. They paused, grunting, but this time the gunfire didn't scare them away.

We turned and ran.

Satina had led Lani through a portal of elephant ear palms and disappeared. Johnny and Dusty were in fast pursuit. I had a glimpse of Satina's bare foot as she pushed Lani out of sight and disappeared. Rocco had seen them and plunged headlong into the foliage. I made the error of pausing to look again down the trail. One of the beast-men hurled a spear with near-deadly accuracy. I dodged, but I still felt that spear cut the air just an inch from my left ear.

A roaring filled the air. Three beast-men were screaming and charged up the hill; the closest being the one who nearly impaled my head with a spear. I shot him with my .45 and he dropped like a sack of barley.

The other two didn't hesitate at all, and they leaped over their comrade's still twitching form, their spears raised and ready to fly. I scrambled around and ran as fast as I could. I don't believe I was breathing; I was just reacting to a sudden desire to stay alive. I didn't know what lay beyond that wall of wavering palms and branches, but I flew into it and came crashing onto a rocky trail so narrow that for a painstaking moment I thought I was trapped and caught up in brambles and twigs. I saw a rocky indentation that crossed upwards on my left and I dashed along, pushing myself hard. There was no one in sight ahead of me. Satina, Lani, Johnny, Dusty and Rocco had disappeared.

I ascended a hill. The trail twisted left, and then a hard right before sloping upwards at a dangerous angle. This is where I had my glimpse of Johnny and Satina helping the others climb to the top of a precipice. They saw me, and Dusty raised a finger to his lips signaling me to remain silent. I didn't require encouragement. I sprinted after them, my thighs aching from my exertions.

I could hear the beast-men behind me, but they seemed further away. Still, I had a sense that somehow they had followed me into the dense greenery and were still on the hunt.

Satina had led my friends up a rocky incline where they used protruding rocks and vines to heave themselves over the ledge. I had begun to ascend the short cliff when I glanced back to see a spear hurtling at my head. I twisted without a second to spare, the spear shattering on the rocks just inches away. I would have been impaled if not for that instinctive glance over my shoulder.

I lost my grip and fell. My momentum carried me to the left, off the trail, and I plunged helplessly into a strand of large palm fronds where I slammed into the mossy earth. At the same instant, the breath was knocked from my lungs, I heard Johnny cut loose with a burst from the Thompson. The percussive thunder shattered the humid morning followed by the tinkle of expended brass raining onto the rocks. I heard the angry jabber of the beast-men nearby.

Forcing myself to my knees, I sucked in air, the black dots still swimming before my eyes. I was out of sight from the trail, which was now above me.

I still had my .45, which I had shoved back into the underarm harness while I climbed. With the gun in my hand, again I only felt incrementally confident. I heard the beast-men poking at the jungle growth looking for me, although they didn't sound as close.

I stumbled to my feet still out of breath, and pressed aside the leaves and vines for a better view. I heard the sea pounding at the shore as I realized the wind had picked up. It was a warm sea breeze scented with spice, which I thought was odd, and before I could gather my thoughts, a beast-man crashed into me with a growl erupting from his misshapen mouth. My gun was knocked from my hand as we tumbled backwards.

His hands were empty until they found my throat. His strength was incredible. For the first time I had a close-up look at this genetic monstrosity. His teeth were broken which gave them the appearance of fangs. His ears were indeed pointed, his mongoloid brow not unlike the skulls of ancient cave dwellers I had seen in the archives of the Natural History Museum. His eyes were strange; black pupils glared at me with hatred. His breath smelled of decaying meat.

Thrashing sideways, I forced his right hand free and held a steady grip on his wrist. I brought my knees up roughly and jammed him in the belly. He didn't let go and his left hand continued to tear at my throat. If he pressed any harder and gained leverage, he would shatter my windpipe.

I experienced a moment of clarity where I realized I was being killed by a man with an intelligence level less than that of a dog. I slammed a knee into his scrotum, which made him howl, and I broke free of his hand. Still gripping his right wrist, I twisted his arm clockwise which turned him over as he bellowed. I had maneuvered above him. With his strength he might have easily killed me had he any intelligence and knew how to fight. It was my good fortune that he was what he appeared; a sad creature born to this world with no chance for something better, and I had to kill him.

I brought my boot down hard on his face with a sickening crunch. Twice more, then a pause, and four more times my boot came down on his face as I gripped his right arm and held him pinned to the ground. I am ashamed that I had to kill him in such an agonizing matter, but I had no choice.

When his body had ceased twitching, I turned away. I nearly retched. Gasping for air, I was dizzy and exhausted. I searched for the .45, found it, and after taking a deep breath, I climbed onto the trail. There were a few bodies on the trail where the Thompson machinegun had done its work. Johnny called down to me.

"Captain, up here! There's one coming up the trail!"

Another brute had seen me and I was no longer in any condition to fight. As the beast-man screamed and ran toward me, I lifted the gun and shot him. Then, tucking my automatic in the holster, I climbed to the ledge without looking back again. Johnny and Rocco pulled me over the ledge and dragged me out of view. The climb hadn't taken very long but as I lay there with my lungs heaving it seemed as if it had taken an eternity to rejoin my crew. Lani kneeled near me with a hand gently on my arm.

"Elliot, I was so worried…"

I wanted to say something clever in return, but all I could manage to do at the time was to pat her arm affectionately. A ridiculous moment if ever I had one.

Rocco pulled me to my feet. Satina said to wait because with all of us out of view the beast-men were confused and would probably leave the area if we didn't make any sound. I agreed that we might wait a few moments before continuing upward. I was done in and craved a shot of bourbon.

"Well, Captain, this is quite a fix we're in," Rocco said. He was grinning like a schoolboy on a holiday. Rocco was loving every minute of this. "And let's not forget that Badoo is out there. No doubt that crazy Zulu bastard will have his hands full like we did."

SEVEN

A few years earlier, I had witnessed Rocco taking on four cannibals in the New Guinea mountain jungle. These cannibals had knocked me senseless, lashed my wrists and legs with vines, and were preparing to skin me alive and cook my flesh. Rocco, being a warrior at heart, demonstrated the joy of possessing an extraordinary fighting ability, which is greatly aided by his six foot four-inch frame, battle tested sinews and his uncannily brilliant Italian mind. Rocco is something of a Renaissance man in the art of violence.

I have previously written of our colorful circumstances, and this journal will rest with the other journals as a record of our crimes and misadventures, all of which Rocco has participated in with a zeal that accepts no boundaries. In short, he is the best man to have at your side when under attack.

Thus far, our circumstances had been perilous enough, but I knew that Rocco sensed an intricate web of deceit, and Rocco's instincts were never wrong.

"The place reeks of trouble," he said bluntly. "Don't forget that freighter you saw. There was something on the wind earlier. We have visitors on this island, more than those bogeymen bastards and more than this Satina's family. I can smell them."

"Once Satina leads us to Lani's father we can get the hell out of here."

"That will take us another day. If we meet him today, we can leave at first light tomorrow. Or we can stay and see what the hell is going on. If your old love Victoria is involved then you know something is wrong here; something that would bring that diamond craving bitch all the way to this tropical hellhole, and I don't have to tell you what trouble she can cause."

Rocco is never shy about voicing his opinion. In fact, Rocco had once recommended that I smother Victoria with a pillow, but not before providing her with an obligatory tryst as befits all men of our stature. He wasn't joking.

"She is a concern," I conceded, "but there's too much here that we don't know yet. Let's hope that Lani's father can shed some light on all of this."

Rocco set his gaze on Satina who was talking with Lani. Johnny stood nearby while Dusty had crept to the cliff's edge to watch for the beast-men.

"She's a beauty, that one is. Johnny's done got himself smitten. I knew a woman whose father owned a vineyard in Provence and she had flashing eyes like that. Her name was Claudia. I never knew a woman with a body like hers. I couldn't get enough of her. A man doesn't mind tangled sheets on his bed with a woman like her under them."

"I don't recall you ever telling me about her. I remember the woman you told me about from Rome."

"She was something, too, but Claudia gave wine a fresh taste. A woman can be a man's salvation, or she can kill him."

"What happened to Claudia?"

"Nothing. I suppose she's quite happy. When her husband found out about us, I was forced to kill him in a duel. It was all quite honorable. She inherited his fortune, sold the vineyard, and bought a villa in Switzerland. She has her pick now of all the Austrians and English boys that ski there on their holidays. I heard she's happy. Can't blame her."

Rocco gave a throaty laugh as he talked, but all the while his eyes were piercing the jungle, alert for any sign of danger.

"You just made that up," I accused him.

"The hell I did. I have a photograph of the bitch somewhere in my gear."
Finally, Rocco took his eyes off the jungle and appraised me. "Now, captain,
if your old bones are rested enough I suggest we get up that hill. This part
of the jungle isn't where I want to be right now."

"Be careful who you call old."

The beast-men appeared to have given up on their search for us, and
Dusty reported that the survivors had removed the bodies of their brethren.
Satina informed us in her fractured English that they would eat the bodies
at a feast that night. As I mentioned, I had encountered cannibals before,
and I hoped they were downwind from us when they began to cook the
bodies.

Satina led us silently into the jungle and followed a winding trail that
took us deeper into the Sumtoan hills. I sensed that we were getting closer
when at length we traversed a broad plain where two large canvas tents
were set up. I had expected to reach the summit where we had spied what
we believed was a city, and this plateau lay in a valley just below that ridge
of verdant hills.

There were several Zebu (*Bos taurus*) grazing upon the grass near the
tents. So astonished was I that I came to halt. We stared in disbelief at
the Zebu because they are not generally indigenous to any tropical island.
I had seen Zebu before, in Southeast Asia, when I worked for an Asian
warlord named Donny Hong. I recognized the Zebu from its droopy ears
and telltale hump on its neck. The obvious fact that they, and perhaps
even the Komodo dragons, had been brought here for some unknown
purpose was a startling revelation. Sumtoa Island was becoming more of
an enigma with each passing moment. The Zebu can be utilized as dairy
cattle or for beef, but a Zebu's dairy output is low compared to an average
bovine. Additionally, I knew the Zebu were especially tolerant of high
temperatures. Having the Zebu logically meant at least a modest dairy
production was evident.

Satina smiled—the girl was always smiling—and she rushed forward
to greet an older woman who emerged from the tent. They spoke to each
other in a Polynesian dialect, and that was when Professor Joseph Kawena
emerged from the tent.

Lani shouted with joy and rushed into her father's arms. Finally, after
a few moments of this emotional reunion, Lani introduced her father. We
shook hands.

Professor Kawena only vaguely resembled his daughter, and as such, I
assumed her features tilted more toward her mother's side. The professor

stood about five feet eight inches tall, an average height. He looked robust and alert. His handshake was firm. His curly dark hair was beginning to show signs of gray. His eyes sparkled and spoke of his academic training and intelligence. I liked him immediately. First impressions are important to me.

"We don't have much time," he said, "but come inside and rest awhile. We have some food, and then we'll have to leave."

The interior of the tent confirmed my conclusion about the dairy production. They had some milk in clay canisters, and some fresh fish that was being cooked over a low fire. Several makeshift cots fashioned from wooden slats offered resting places. We sat on wooden benches and waited for the food to cook while drinking fresh milk. Rocco, being diplomatic, drank the milk although I knew he much preferred a swig from the bourbon he kept in his flask. Johnny sat with Satina, and Dusty stretched out on the floor. Lani's expression was one of relief. It was as if a great burden had been lifted from her shoulders now that we had located her father, and her relaxed demeanor was an entirely new perspective. That she is beautiful is not in question, but seeing her happy was a new experience, and one that I determined at that moment to maintain at all costs.

"I have to tell you I was relieved when Satina reported your arrival. She had seen a photograph I have of Lani and knew immediately who she was. I came down last night from the village. In a little while, we'll hike back up. We can't stay here."

"Will those beast-men come looking for us?" I inquired.

"Oh no, not them. By the way, that clan is indigenous to this island. I'm afraid their low mental capacity is the result of centuries of inbreeding."

"That's incredible. You're saying they never had any social structure?"

"If they did it's so far in the past that we'll never know. The best that I can speculate is inbreeding was constant, and their race will die out in a few years. Inbreeding weakens the immune system. There are but three females left, all rather old and beyond child bearing. They don't know this, of course, because their intelligence threshold is lower than any primate."

I suddenly had so many questions for professor Kawena that my mind was reeling. "They live to eat, sleep and procreate then, that's all? How do they gather food? Is there any chief or authority figure among them?"

Professor Kawena chuckled. "I can see that your reputation with the Natural History Museum is well deserved. You have a perceptive mind."

I was flattered that the professor had heard of me at all, but anxious for answers to my questions. The professor removed a pipe from a canvas bag that was attached to his belt, including a small pouch of tobacco. He patted the tobacco into the pipe, snapped a match to life, and puffed at the pipe until a small cloud of blue smoke materialized above his head like a wavering question mark.

"Satina's people, this tribe, are Polynesian travelers," he continued, "and they have been here approximately sixty years. Those beast-men, as you call them, are called Uhaite. I am uncertain as to their name's etymology. It's probably a Polynesian derivative of their original Chinese name."

I was astounded. "Chinese? I noticed they possessed exaggerated Mongolian features."

"That's the least of it really. I assume that your ship can accommodate guests?"

"Of course, we'll leave in the morning."

"And do you possess radio transmission?"

"Yes, once we're in range of another vessel or radio tower."

"Excellent, but before we can leave I'm afraid we'll need to overcome several challenges."

"My crew here can handle anything."

"Let's hope so. You see, there are several number of people interested in the treasure, and then there are the pirates to deal with."

"Hold on," I said, "you're going too fast. What treasure and what people are after it? And what pirates are you talking about?"

The professor was pensive a moment. He certainly had our attention.

"Yes, it is a lot to take in at once. I apologize."

"Father, are these the red diamonds that you mentioned in your letter?" Lani had gripped her father's arm in her excitement.

"Red diamonds? Oh, yes, and more. There are emeralds, rubies and gold, a few sapphires, and I believe a portion of silver coins."

I cannot adequately describe my astonishment at hearing this news. Everything that the professor was telling us might have sounded like a fantasy from one of the pulp magazines we kept in the salon below deck. Before I could utter another question, a man entered the tent; he was older and short but muscular. By all assessments this man, and all of this wayward Polynesian group, were fit and capable people. He spoke to the woman we had first seen in that fractured Polynesian dialect, and then they spoke with the professor. Lani understood some of what they were saying. I saw the concern darken her brow. The professor and Lani rose to their feet.

"We're leaving now," the professor said. "I'll explain along the way."

Then to my already tested amazement, the man pulled a flintlock rifle from beneath a swath of animal furs near one of the benches. We exited the tent hastily, and the professor immediately led us up a trail past the grazing Zebu. The man with the flintlock rifle remained behind, as did the woman. We ascended a steep grassy incline that proved two things: first, I was not conditioned properly for mountain climbing, and two, Rocco showed no sign of fatigue and proved he was in better shape than all of us save the Polynesians. Although the professor had stated that he would explain more to us; our ascent necessitated that we concentrate on the task at hand. Our climb was carried out in silence.

The rolling hills soon gave way to a thickly forested area, primarily flowering jungle brush and small trees. We zig-zagged higher into the hills, and less than two hours later we came in view of the hillside village. The narrow square dwellings were made of mud, stone and perhaps some improvised stucco type substance. I immediately noted that some of the doors, which were cut from wood, were painted red, white and blue in an alternating fashion. This reminded me that in Tibet red was significant of a Buddhist temple. In fact, I would soon learn that these Polynesians practiced a hybrid form of Buddhism.

Professor Kawena quickly ushered us along a narrow street where we followed him through one of the blue doors. The interior was sparsely furnished, but just getting out of the blistering heat was a relief. The chairs and tables were made from wood and the craftsmanship was quite impressive. This was our introduction to the Sumtoan Polynesians. We drank fresh water and ate again (more fish), and were treated to some biscuits that were very good. We were introduced to an elderly man named Vaea. He had a white beard and piercing dark eyes. Vaea was the eldest tribal member, and apparently the ruling voice. His assistant was his son, age approximately fifteen, named Turoa. Vaea had a young and beautiful wife named Oleka whose sole purpose was to bear children for the aging king.

It was in this room, and not thirty minutes after our arrival, that two significant events occurred that I must document. The first was the arrival of another of Vaea's sons, Rarahu, age about thirty, who resembled his father in every way except age. The second was an introduction to a young female named Tehani. That I—and all of us—would come to care so much for these people in such a short period of time is that part of this narrative where I may falter. Whatever words I scrawl across the pages of this journal

Vaea was the eldest tribal member...

are inadequate, but I am compelled to make the effort.

Tehani rivals Lani and Satina in beauty. She is Satina's cousin, and in this instant Dusty fell immediately in love with her. Rarahu was the bravest man I have ever met. Although I have given due credit to my crew, also brave men, it is Rarahu who shall remain forever a great hero in my mind.

Rarahu and Tehani spoke some English while Vaea did not. They welcomed us warmly and assured us not to worry. "We have plenty musket ball and powder," Rarahu said. Looking at Professor Kawena for guidance, we were at last, given the startling details of our predicament.

"When I arrived here last year my immediate concern was identifying the source of the red diamonds which had been brought to my attention by an adjunct professor of anthropology, Simon McCallister, who at the time was suffering from a heart ailment. In fact, the old man passed away not long after this. I had received from him a very small fragment of red diamond with a letter stating that it was sent to him by a man named Thad Bellamy who wanted to ascertain its authenticity." Professor Kawena paused and packed fresh tobacco into his pipe, puffing contentedly a moment as we all waited for him to continue. "Simon was an expert on rare gemstones and a good friend of mine. Now, the crucial thing about this diamond fragment being that it was not only real, but reportedly from a diamond mining operation on Sumtoa Island. Naturally, I was suspicious knowing that Sumtoa is the remnant of an ancient volcanic eruption much as was Krakatoa and Bora Bora. These are ancient land structures in the Pacific, and certainly hardly the place where geology encourages diamond formation."

Professor Kawena's voice had taken on the tone of a skilled orator and I could easily see the passion and knowledge that burned like a fire in his eyes.

"Frankly, I suspected that Mr. Bellamy was an unscrupulous character, and that suspicion has proven to be true. The only thing that I could verify with any certainty was that Sumtoa Island was the subject of a mining operation funded by your friend, Miss Victoria Ransom. Again, it is impossible for diamond formation of this type on the geologic land mass known as Sumtoa Island. The very idea is absurd; so I set out to discover what was going on. The university had allowed me a few weeks off, but this has sadly turned into something that is quite above my capabilities, which is why your timely arrival is of the utmost importance."

"I don't understand," I interjected, "you mentioned a treasure and pirates?"

"Indeed I did. The treasure is quite real, and so are the pirates." The professor stood up. "I suppose it's best if I simply show you as I explain everything. It's quite complicated."

Rarahu, who spoke in the same fractured English as Satina, said, "The men are ready. Follow us."

I instructed Dusty to remain behind, as did Johnny who by now wasn't paying much attention because of Satina's presence. Both Dusty and Johnny found themselves content in paradise with young girls like Satina and Tehani giggling softly and tossing bright glances in their direction. Lani stayed close to her father as Rocco and I followed them into a street that wound upwards through the village.

Out in the street, we were joined by six men with flintlock rifles. The profusion of rifles was surprising and, judging by the looks of these men, they knew how to shoot. A flintlock rifle is heavy, and shooting it accurately requires a great deal of practice. Here is one of the anomalies of the Sumtoan Polynesians. I was eager to hear Professor Kawena's explanation for everything that we had seen.

The narrow winding street was barely wide enough for three men side by side, and each side of the street crowded with box dwellings, some of which were but crude stone, mud and wood construction. Again, I noticed the colored doorways, but before I could inquire further the street ended. I realized that from the valley below that this winding street and double row of buildings had created an optical illusion. The village was much smaller than it appeared and the dwellings were much smaller. From a distance, this overlapping offered the appearance of a staggered row of buildings when in fact they were two rows of squat structures at slightly different elevations.

We had come up against a cliff-face and the street was dead-ended. Before us was a faded red door. Two men with rifles entered first and I glimpsed them lighting torches. Professor Kawena gestured for us to follow.

"The red doors indicate a religious temple," the professor explained. "The blue doors are family homes or sleeping quarters, and the white doors designate storage facilities. Their religion is an interesting combination of Buddhism and sun worship that must have developed as a result of their environment. Most interesting to me was the moon pool ritual which you may witness tonight."

Inside the room there was a long wooden table bearing a jade Buddha and various other artifacts that surprised me. They had lit candles as well and the room was soon bathed in a yellow glow. Rocco had his eyes on the jade Buddha. There were golden candleholders, albeit slightly tarnished and layered with dust. There were clay tablets bearing Chinese symbols on the table similar to the ones we had recovered from the Christian dwelling in the lowlands.

With a thousand questions poised on my lips, the professor said abruptly, "The treasure is above us. We'll have to climb."

At first we were confused, but when the professor moved to his left carrying a small torch, I noticed rungs had been set in the wall like a ladder. Glancing up I saw the black chasm. In seconds he had heaved himself up and another second passed and the darkness above came alive with the torch's flare. Lani followed then Rocco and I. Interestingly enough, the riflemen remained in the room below, and they had shut the outside door.

Professor Kawena lit a few additional torches, and we saw the treasure. Treasure in heaps and mounds, glittering gold and mounds of golden and silver coins. On a small table a pile of red diamonds, its value inestimable. Overflowing in an ancient trunk with tarnished brass hinges, the sides layered with cobwebs, did lie emeralds, polished yet crudely cut and still immensely valuable. I saw a diamond necklace and sapphire wrist ornaments. Rubies gleamed dully from beneath a skin of dust. There was but for a few seconds no sound other than the torches' flames sucking greedily at the stale air and crackling with spectral mirth.

Herein we found the wealth of Kublai Khan. Here lay the fabled riches of El Dorado or Shangri-La. Here then, too, was Blackbeard's fabled loot, a buccaneer's payment in precious gems. Old King Solomon's treasure could not be envisioned by the greatest of pulp writers fevered with liquor and scratching out their vision with ink on a goosequill pen. This was a rarity of riches; a dream of a kingdom unknown to history.

Professor Kawena's voice was now but a whisper, but we all heard him.

"I'll bring your attention to the Chinese markings on the gold coins, and scattered here and there on certain pieces of jewelry. This treasure must certainly have been gathered over many decades, which offers a conundrum. However, thanks to the late Simon McCallister, whose notes I read, I believe everything here originated with Zheng Shi, the so-called lady pirate of China. There's scant knowledge of her activities that's verified, but we do know that she organized a red flag fleet of pirates and exerted her rule over the South China Sea. In approximately 1807 the elder rulers of the Qing Dynasty determined to usurp her rule in conjunction with a plot orchestrated by both British and Portuguese spies, but that coup failed." The professor paused and pointed to a badly damaged mural painted on the cave wall. "I believe this is one of her treasure hordes. These pictographs tell a specific story. How many other treasures of Zheng Shi will ever be known to us? This is all unverified, but no doubt those red diamonds were plunder from a foreign ship whose tale is lost in time."

Lani had picked up a silver coin and was intent on its features. "Father, some of these coins have Chinese symbols, but some also bear Roman markings."

"That's very perceptive of you," the professor smiled. He was barely able to contain the pride in his voice as Lani turned the coin over in her hands. "We'll never know how Zheng Shi obtained those coins, but here they are. It seems impossible, I know. This collection of ancient Chinese loot, Roman coins, some French golden candelabras, and perhaps some Greek coins as well, it fairly boggles the mind."

"This is a sestertius bearing the image of Marcus Aurelius, and this one has an image of Nero," Lani said. The excitement in her voice was palpable. "Father, I've never seen Roman coins in such good condition!"

"Precisely. The long stretch of time has shown us a mystery that may never be solved. What I can tell you is that the descendants of Zheng Shi are intent on retrieving this treasure, and thanks to Victoria Ransom these modern-day pirates have come to Sumtoa to take it, and I'm afraid they will stop at nothing to get it."

Then, as if guided by the illicit hand of some dark god, we heard the nearby sound of gunfire followed by agitated shouts from the Sumtoan riflemen down below.

EIGHT

"We have to move!" the professor rasped as he lifted his blazing torch. "Follow me along this path!"

On the far left, the cavern narrowed into a long thin tunnel that curved upwards. Rocco moved up behind the professor with his gun in hand. We traveled approximately thirty-five feet into the cold, stygian darkness before the tunnel widened. Far ahead, I glimpsed a sliver of light. We paused momentarily, and Lani pressed her warm, lithe body next to mine. She was trembling slightly, and I could smell the sea breeze in her hair. Gently, I took her into my arms. Her pulse was racing.

"There's an exit here," the professor explained, "but we have to be careful. The ledge outside is quite narrow."

"Does this exit on the western side of the island?" Rocco asked.

"Yes, and from here we can circle down back to the village."

We exited the cavern onto the volcanic ledge. Our view of the far northwestern side of Sumtoa included the rocky escarpment where we had previously noted the pier. The freighter that we had seen was about a mile away, and down near the dock we saw two large motorboats lashed to the pilings. Of equal interest was the one hundred ton sloop that lay at anchor closer to the island. The sloop's rapier-like bowsprit was nearly as long as the hull, its single-mast and square topsail providing it with a hearty wind that could propel her easily at eleven knots. There was cannon visible upon her deck. A small flag bearing Chinese symbols caught the breeze and fluttered like a black bird atop the rigging.

A distant volley of gunfire caught our attention, behind us and down near the village.

"Miss Ransom had warned us some months ago that she would come back, and she has." The professor led us along the ledge to our left as he spoke. "It's a complicated mess, really. Rumors circulated for centuries and passed down as fables and folklore that such a treasure existed. The existence of an organized group of Zheng Shi's descendants, or at least people claiming such lineage, had convinced my friend professor McCallister, that the sudden profusion of red diamonds in the South China Sea was the result of a treasure discovery. In that regard he was correct."

There was a pause and for a moment, we stood on a narrow precipice as I realized we were visible to anyone with binoculars scanning the cliffside from those ships. We had to press our backs against the wall and inch down the ledge, and, frankly, if I had known in advance of the danger this posed to us, and especially to Lani, I would have insisted we return the way we came. However, professor Kawena moved with expertise and apparently without fear, nimble as a cougar. Rounding a corner, we were finally out of sight, not that it mattered all that much.

"Professor, who is attacking the village now? Are they Chinese pirates or Victoria Ransom's men?"

"Well, captain, I'm afraid it's a combination of both. It was Miss Ransom that contacted the Zheng Shi cult, and they are certainly a cult no matter if their lineage is proven. She had attempted to negotiate with the Sumtoans to no avail. The treasure has become a part of their survival. With it, they have existed all these years and used a small portion of treasure to fund medical supplies, clothing and some food. But nothing lasts forever. Once they made the mistake of bartering with a red diamond, they set in motion a series of communications and events that may have resulted in professor McCallister's death. It also resulted in the appearance of Miss Ransom whom I have determined is the equal in evil to only Satan himself. Miss Ransom initially thought the gemstones could be mined, but then she found out it was all actually a lost treasure."

The trail dropped steeply and we found ourselves in a dense stretch of palms and vines. Several more bursts of gunfire occurred; a combination of flintlock rifles and some small arms fire from a revolver.

We emerged onto another ledge, this one looking out on the valley below the village, and adjacent to the village by just a few meters, I saw several Chinese looking up at us. They had Japanese rifles, the Meiji 38 or Arisaka rifle, probably bought on the black market. The Japanese wouldn't knowingly sell the Chinese their rifles. I counted a dozen men, and none of them looked frightened. They were lounging about and smoking, well out of range of Rarahu's flintlock bearing riflemen. One of them watched us through a small brass telescope. He was bald and wearing an armless shirt that showed off the snake tattoos on his forearms. He had a goatee and a long thin mustache that curled down past his chin. He looked like a mandarin or some Hollywood villain.

I couldn't see them from this angle, but I knew that Dusty and Johnny were down there getting a feel for what was happening. I expected they would stay out of sight, and I was equally confident that Rarahu would command their actions accordingly. The Chinese may or may not have known of our presence, and I assumed that they did. *The Reaper's Scythe* wouldn't be missed by any curious travelers circumnavigating Sumtoa.

Rocco, intuitive as ever, said as if reading my mind. "We need to assume that the lovely Miss Victoria has tipped them off as to our numbers, types of firearms and capabilities."

"Which explains why they're feeling us out."

"Once they get a sense of where everything is, they can rush us and expect to overpower us."

"We haven't heard any shooting from the ship," I said, "but I don't want to assume that Doc and Edgar are safe."

"That Zulu magic man is out there, so we have him."

"I pity the enemy that meet him next."

"Remember that Laurel and Hardy picture we saw in Brisbane a few years ago?"

I glanced at Rocco. He came up with odd things to say at the most unusual times. "Sure, *Sons of the Pioneers* or something like that."

"Do you remember what the fat one said?"

"The fat one? That's Ollie, right?"

"Well, here's another nice mess you've gotten me into. That's what he said."

"It sure as hell is a mess," I agreed.

The Chinese man with the telescope had put the telescope away. He was talking with some of the other men. A few of them moved off in different directions. I couldn't see where they had gone, but it didn't matter, because we knew where they were going, and this small volcanic island suddenly felt much smaller.

A few minutes later, we entered the village and I asked the professor to take Lani inside and stay out of sight. He didn't say anything, but the look on his face spoke volumes. He was relying on me, and on my crew, to make everything right. I prayed that I was up to the task.

Rocco conversed with Dusty who was insistent, quite naturally, that a broken wing never stopped an eagle from attempting to fly, and he swore in the name of General Ulysses S. Grant that he'd die before letting anything happen to such beautiful girls as Tehani and Satina. I didn't require any convincing that the young Oklahoman would handle himself well, so with a quick glance at Rocco, we let it go. Dusty would position himself in a small doorway, and fire on any intruders that came into view if they made it that far up the street. He mentioned with a wide grin that it wouldn't be hard "to pick out the slanty eyed bastards" when he saw them.

Rarahu had positioned three riflemen at the edge of the road, where the village began its upward slope. The danger here being the immense jungle that spread out into a rolling section of nearly impenetrable hills. Once the Chinese pirates climbed that ledge where I had nearly been impaled by a spear, they could scatter into the jungle, which gave them a tactical advantage.

We had to stop the pirates as they came over the ledge. I asked Rarahu if I could position Johnny with his Thompson at the front line, and to my amazement, he declined.

"We need big guns later," he said, "not now. We wait."

"He's right," Rocco said, rubbing it in, "let them play this out while I snoop around."

For Rocco snooping around meant getting into trouble and since Rarahu was confident he had things under control, I followed Rocco.

"Something's not right, captain," Rocco was saying as he walked up the sloping road toward that part of the village that buttressed the cliffs, and where the treasure cave was hidden behind the façade of a small building. "Chinese aren't stupid or suicidal. Sending men up the main road is a distraction."

"Are you proposing they're scaling the exterior wall up here?"

"Either that or they've found another way in."

But there was nothing there save a lonely breeze and sunlight. I looked down the narrow road and the buildings seemed forlorn and abandoned although I knew the older Polynesians and the women were hiding inside. Rocco was right, there was something wrong; something that we had missed.

"All right," I said, "so they've found another way in, but where?"

It had grown quiet, but at that instant as if guided by a providential hand, we heard the distant call of a wild gull, hardly noticeable, and we turned to stare past the buildings at the jungle palms swaying in that haunting breeze down the road. Rocco raised an eyebrow.

They hadn't scaled the cliff or attempted to climb over that ledge where the road began. Somehow they had come up into the jungle and found a way into that rolling section of dense vines and twisted trees. If they made it through that wall of foliage, they could climb over the first five or six small buildings and come at us from the village itself. If they were smart, and I assumed they were, another group could then climb the ledge and rush us from the road and thus provide a tactical advantage of hitting us from two directions. We didn't have enough men to withstand such an attack.

We found Rarahu and told him. He nodded grimly. "There's a small trail there," he said, pointing, "that leads to our pool of stars. They must pass it to get here. There's no other way."

We didn't have time to ask what pool of stars he was talking about. Rocco and I squeezed into an alley between two buildings and found ourselves in the jungle just before that volcanic layer of boulders began its jagged ascent. We found the well-worn trail that curved downhill toward the switchback and ledge where I had nearly met my forefathers. After about fifty feet, the path curved inward toward the densest concentration of jungle at this elevation. Beyond that and before us lie a rolling swath of trees and brush. This unseen jungle valley was alive with insects, persistent heat, and the heady scent of moss, decay and strange blooming flowers.

The path was well worn but the elephant ear leaves and tangled brush crowded our shoulders as we pushed into a sweltering green world. By the time we reached a small circular clearing, we were drenched in sweat. There was a round stone bowl set on a handmade pedestal, and around the clearing were crudely fashioned wood benches. This was the area Rarahu had referred to as the pool of stars.

We heard a boot crunch onto some brambles and deciduous twigs. Rocco drifted left and eased himself into a canopy of brush. I stepped out of the clearing on our right, pressing myself low and trying to cover myself with branches. I had just finished moving when a brute of a man suddenly crashed into the clearing. He was short but built like a rhinoceros. His bald head gleamed with sweat, his thick legs were corded with muscle, as were his arms and broad shoulders. His pants were sailor trousers, cut-off at the knees, and he wore sandals. His shirt was a sleeveless tunic; gray and stained from god knows what. The insects that buzzed around his sweating head didn't bother him at all. He held an Arisaka rifle in his stubby hands.

He came into the clearing grunting like a hog, his beady eyes staring in perplexity at the stone bowl. He set the rifle against the pedestal and fished into his pocket for his tobacco pouch. We watched as he rolled himself a cigarette, and when the match flared to life and he took his first puff, Rocco decided to kill him.

It was a horrible scene, enacted with cold precision, a silent pantomime of death played out in a cloud of agitated black insects. Rocco came up behind him with his jack-knife in hand and slashed at the brute's jugular vein. I saw the blood jettison, but the man turned and struck a mighty blow at Rocco's head. A rhinoceros is not easy to kill.

The man flung his hammy fist at Rocco's head three more times in rapid succession. The blows sent Rocco reeling. The gush of blood at the pirate's neck had diminished somewhat although he was still bleeding profusely.

Rocco struck again with the knife but the brute was fast. He dodged, and in a remarkably swift movement, he kicked Rocco in the balls, which dropped him to his knees. Lunging down, the Chinaman pummeled Rocco with his fists, striking so fast that his hands were a blur. Although we didn't care to use our guns just yet because it would destroy the element of surprise (our solitary tactical advantage) I was about to level the Chinaman with my .45 when Rocco sprang upwards and drove the short blade deep into the man's heart.

A guttural oath flung from his lips as he stared down at the embedded blade. Rocco's own enormous strength had buried the jack-knife to the hilt, a crimson flower spreading over the man's chest. The loss of blood from the neck wound and decisive fatal blow had literally stopped the man in his tracks. He stood there dumbly staring at Rocco, but his eyes could no longer see. He stood like a statue with his hands at his sides, his lips mumbling some incomprehensible Chinese gibberish, and then he toppled facedown, twitched, and fought no more.

I was conscious of the droning of hundreds of insects, which descended upon the body like a pestilence. How swiftly nature reacts to the dead. Rocco was breathing heavy and looked perturbed.

"Why, that bugger almost had me!" was all he said.

Rocco took the Arisaka rifle. The Arisaka has a five-round magazine and Rocco found a few extra cartridges in the corpse's pockets, but no identification papers. Other than the tobacco and the extra cartridges, the pirate had been traveling light.

We decided to go in the direction from which the brute had come, and after a struggle in the greenery, we emerged on the opposite side of the clearing where the earth sloped sharply downwards. We could see possibly thirty feet in every direction, which wasn't nearly enough. We knew there were more of them, and we knew they would kill us in an instant if they saw us. There would be no second chances, no reprieves.

Under any other circumstances, I might have paused and photograph-ed the jungle as the sun slanted down through the palms. The jungle is a truly frightening but beautiful landscape, and it is decidedly unfriendly when populated by Chinese pirates. Perhaps the scientist in me at times predominates my character, because as we progressed I noticed the profusion of littoral plants. A pacific island does not nurture the opportunity for survival, and plants and animals here must survive extraordinary circumstances upon their arrival. The seeds come on the wind or are dropped by birds, the animals must surely come with men on ships, save for those endless mysteries of the seven seas that spawn creatures whose origins are yet unknown, such as the Komodo dragons. Rocco was still on my left and we made slow progress as we edged toward a thin ravine. I didn't like it because I was feeling boxed in.

We were halfway down the slope when we saw a man slip into a strangle-hold of scrub and small banyan trees. He was across from us, coming down the opposite slope, and he hadn't seen us.

A rifle thundered, its report shattering the stillness.

I felt the bullet cut the air just millimeters from my head, and followed by another shot. By then I was tucked low, and holding my fire. In my peripheral vision, I saw Rocco on his knees in a shooter's stance and aiming off to my right. Turning in that direction I saw two more men, and one of them had his rifle aimed at me. Rocco's rifle boomed and the man's head disappeared in a cloud of red and gray mist. I heard Chinese curses and shouts of alarm.

Both Chinese pirates dodged for cover. They were separated on the opposite hillside by forty yards, and from his crouched position, Rocco twisted the Arisaka lever and filled the breech, his lips turned up in a wicked smile. I saw the muzzle flash as the blue smoke wafted upwards. A man fell, screaming. Rocco swept to his right, but I had lost sight of the other man.

Rocco hadn't lost sight of the man, however, and he fired at a clump of *Croton insularis*, the fanning silver croton, his rifle booming. We knew his bullet had struck its mark because we heard it thud into the body. We could hear the man's gurgling death rattle even though we couldn't see him. We found the body lying face-up in a cluster of purple and orange wildflowers. I took the dead man's rifle and the cartridges from his pocket.

Neither Rocco nor I enjoyed the prospect of ascending that second slope, but the emerging cacophony of gunfire from the village marked the onset of the fight, and there was no turning back. Our presence in the jungle was known, and we expected heavy resistance. We followed a meandering ridge of rocks uphill, alert for sounds or movement. Several times we encountered snarls of vines and up-ended trees that forced us to circle farther out to our left, expecting at any moment that we would encounter the enemy.

It took us twenty minutes to make our way up the thorny ridge, and when we ascended the hill, we had our hands full. I was soaked with so much sweat it was as if I had plunged into a pond and soaked myself. My stomach was a bundle of knots. Eight Chinese pirates were spread out in single-file from left to left to right and advancing on the ridge. They spotted us immediately and opened fire.

I let myself fall to the left hoping that the ground swell would shield me, and it nearly did. In fact, the move saved my life, but one of the bullets clipped my right arm, tearing through muscle. Even with an Arisaka rifle in hand, I was a sitting duck for any long-range riflemen.

I was pressed flat on the ground. I heard Rocco firing and the jabbering of the Chinese pirates as they dove for cover. I rolled left which succeeded in covering my damp body with leafage and mulch. Rocco fired again and I heard a man howl in pain. Lifting my head, I had a view of a man

...one of the bullets clipped my right arm.

crouching near a silver lady dwarf fern, as he lifted his rifle. By the time he fired, I had leveled my sights on him and I pulled the trigger. My bullet struck him, but I couldn't tell if he was dead or merely injured.

A fusillade of rifle fire cut apart the brush surrounding me. The air filled with specks of shattered trees and leaves. I rose up and ran in a crouch, dodging between trees just as a burst of gunfire stitched holes in the ground near me. There were shouts and curses, some garbled, and at least one from a man in pain. Rocco was laying into them from somewhere on the far left.

I was exhausted and my wounded arm was throbbing. I could smell my own blood. Little black insects swarmed in the air around me.

Nearly falling down another slope, I encountered a gurgling stream and stopped. Angry birdsongs chattered from the trees and the sun-laden jungle and hills offered a scene of tranquility, but still my senses warned me of danger.

I scrutinized the jungle. Eventually, I saw a man moving about a hundred yards up a small hill. Slowly, I shifted my position, still keeping low. From a sitting position with my elbow braced against my raised knee, I sighted down the barrel and drew a bead on the man. I heard the man yowling in agony after I shot him.

A flurry of bullets was suddenly ripping apart the foliage next to me. Once more I dodged and crouched-crawled my way backwards in the most unflattering manner, and flattened myself behind a moldy tree. I had a sense where the men were that were firing at me and I was forced to take a dangerous gamble.

I stepped out from behind the tree and took aim, firing rapidly, the rifle hot to the touch. I put two bullets in one man and clipped another in the shoulder; which sent a geyser of blood into the air as the man screamed and went down. Another shot staggered a man backwards, his shirt stained. The man's wailing must have frightened one of the other men who turned and ran. I shot him in the head. The sound of gunfire echoed across the jungle. Nearby, I heard the boom of Rocco's gun.

My intention was to crawl into a better position and take pot-shots at the pirates, but the profusion of currant trees and elephant leaf shrubs made it impossible for me to pinpoint any one pirate's location. To make matters worse, they appeared to know precisely where I was, at least judging from the volume of bullets that were careening in my direction.

There is no position as fatal as a prone one without adequate cover when the enemy has spotted you. Eyeing an overgrown hump of swamp lily, I rolled into it and snaked deeper into the greenery. There was nothing heroic about my actions. I fully expected to be killed at any moment, and I was desperate.

A volcanic rumble shook the jungle floor; the strongest tremor we had experienced thus far. This had the effect of causing the Chinese pirates to shout excitedly, which encouraged Rocco to commence firing. Pushing with my elbows and knees, I managed to traverse fifteen yards as a series of deep rumbles dispersed across the island.

I heard Chinese voices nearby. I stood up and shot the first man I saw. A red mist exploded on the man's head as the bullet struck home. I paused and took time to check the rifle. I finally set eyes on Rocco again. He was closer to me than I had expected, just twenty feet up on my right. He was grinning at me from a crouched position amidst a cluster of white and pale green plants, a *Pseuderanthemum*, and much larger than I had seen before. The dash of pink in the leaves may have been blood or a stem. I gave Rocco a thumbs-up.

Then I saw the remaining Chinese pirates charging us, their rifles spitting smoke as the gunfire echoed across the rolling gulley. It was at this moment that Badoo leapt out from behind a wall of pink and green bamboo orchids with the Thompson sub-machinegun spraying a lethal burst of flame and death at the stunned pirates.

NINE

Badoo would tell me later what happened at the ship. The morning of our departure, an eerie silence descended upon the bay, and he kept a wary eye on the turquoise water for any sign of the Kraken. Knowing that he had seriously injured the beast offered a level of satisfaction, and while he thought the Kraken was sufficiently injured to dissuade any further surfacing, he also accepted that such beasts are unpredictable.

There was little wind. The hot sun burned away the morning mist and the inlet was calm. Badoo was thinking about the African plain of his youth, and the first time his father had tracked a great lion with him. The hot, still air reminded him of Africa. Badoo wondered what his father would say one day when he returned with stories about the Pacific and tales of the faraway islands. He would be careful to state the facts simply and in a manner that his father might not be offended, that Badoo had shown courage against his adversaries. His father was proud man and a fierce warrior.

As a boy he had listened to his father talk about the battle at Isandlwana on the day of a solar eclipse, and the following battle at Rorke's Drift in 1879. The Zulu fought with *assegai*, iron-tipped spears, and with cowhide shields against the red-suits with their rifles. Many Zulu died, but just as many red-suits perished, but these victories meant the end, eventually, for Zulu dominance over their homes. Badoo learned from these tales that how a man lives is equally as important as how he dies.

Badoo once explained to me that a Zulu has more than one name. In fact, he had several names, but his earliest names were Bhekithemba Njabula, and that he was named by his father in a sentimental moment. His name translated, roughly, as to seek hope and to love. His mother had died in childbirth, and his name represented what his father perceived his mother's wishes for her child. "Badoo" was a crude English derivative of "The Bad Duke," tagged onto him by the heavily accented Celtic seamen aboard his first ship, a freighter, and originated from their inability to pronounce his given Zulu names. With his regal bearing, the Celts said he reminded them of a Duke, and a dangerous one at that. Bhekithemba thought Badoo was as good a name as any. He was just Badoo, and if that was good enough for his shipmates, then he allowed it to stand.

He studied the ever-changing light on the water; and he listened to the warm air. What subtle breeze he may have detected was one only his finely wrought senses could discern. There were mysteries on the wind, and omens that came to him as spiced scents on the breeze, or even a telltale sound carried for miles and miles. In this fashion, he recognized that they were not alone. There was another ship, of that he was certain. But his senses had failed to pick out relevant details. He had seen nothing, but he sensed it.

He was not surprised when he heard the distant sound of gunfire. With a burlap sack of some modest provisions, he set out with the Thompson sub-machinegun, leaving the rowboat pulled up and hidden inside an explosion of ferns. He had not gone ten feet into the jungle when a sound caught his attention. He turned back, and watched a small but well-armed group of Chinese pirates board *The Reaper's Scythe* and take Doc and Edgar prisoner.

Mere minutes had prevented his own capture, or more likely, his death. Badoo would not be taken so easily. As it was, Doc and Edgar had fired a few rounds, but quickly surrendered when they realized they were outgunned.

Their choice was wise. They knew that Rocco and I would make certain these pirates faced a reckoning. Badoo watched without emotion, counting men, and assessing each man's strength and weaknesses. From Badoo's perspective, a man was easier to conquer than a hungry and angry lion at a full-charge. These pirates were all formidable men, but they were no lions.

There was one additional incident that he witnessed with great interest. The pirates departed in a long-rowboat, cutting out of the bay with a practiced speed and agility that he found impressive. All the more interesting is that within a few minutes of their departure, a shadow clouded the turquoise bay, and a solitary, exploratory tentacle broke the surface, and slid swiftly again out of sight.

Badoo frowned. What the gods planned for them was unfathomable, but Badoo considered the journey a true test of his abilities, and he relished each moment. Following the trail was easy enough. Contrary to the white man's belief, not all of Africa is a flat, arid place. It's true the upland savannah of KwaZulu-Natal was flat and dry, but most of the Zulu nation included mountainous regions, subtropical thickets and deep, dangerous ravines. Badoo had hunted in the Knysna Forest and spent many nights in the Mngeni River Valley. The Tugela River was also known to him, and these places were as mysterious and as alive as any Pacific island he had visited.

He could track any man and most animals. Only the small, yellow snakes of the African grasslands were difficult to follow. However, they were not poisonous, only deceptive, and quick to hide. He was immediately at ease in the Sumtoan jungle.

When he reached the ancient hut of the long dead Christian, he circled the area studying the ground. From this he learned that we had moved on, and our path was fairly easy to find. We had, at that time, made no effort to hide our progress.

Badoo smelled the Komodo dragons before he saw them. Having encountered these reptiles before, he knew precisely how to avoid them; and he also knew how dangerous these animals could be. He followed our circuitous path around the marshland, and finally began the trek into the hills. The beast-men, or Uhaite, as the professor called them, were enough to give Badoo reason to pause. Here was an unknown factor, and Badoo understood that an unknown variable in dangerous situations could prove to be a man's undoing. Badoo decided to camp in secret, to wait, and to observe.

Badoo later heard the gunfire and sounds of our escape from the Uhaite.

This served to not only help Badoo pin-point our location and direction, but to assess the fighting capabilities of the Uhaite. Badoo arrived at the same conclusion as Rocco and I, namely, the beast-men were physically dangerous but intellectually inept. They were truly ignorant beasts.

Badoo also decided that the Uhaite were evil creatures. Badoo made no apologies later for his actions, not that he had to. For Badoo, the natural world has many layers, including a spiritual layer that I cannot pretend to fathom. He lost himself in darkness, silent as the mist, moving with an inner sight. An island is a promontory, a fragment from the eruption of chaos that witnessed the creation of life. The sea is a part of it; a consuming element that surrounds it, devours it. The molten lava is cooled by the waters that are endless. Phantoms walk the earth in darkness; denizens of other worlds and spirits no earthly religion has yet defined.

He walked in darkness first as a Zulu warrior, and he walked in darkness as a spiritual being in concert with others unknown to mankind. They are here, he told me, with us eternally, and they sail the seven seas in mighty ships cut and fashioned from the trees in ancient forests long before Troglodytes walked the earth.

He found the Uhaite village on the eastern slope of a volcanic foothill. Beneath his feet he detected the rumblings of the Sumtoan volcano, imperceptible to the average person, save for those increasing seismic quakes we had already experienced. Badoo read the message in the land, and with this tool, he understood the value of time.

His first order of business was to procure a spear from the Uhaite. This was easily managed by waiting in the darkness for an opportunity. The Uhaite had constructed crude huts and spent most of the evening cooking small animals over a fire. They chanted and sang, and after eating, many of them slept. A few of them procreated with one of the females, a horrific creature of malformed genetics. Their spears were set up against one of the huts, and Badoo secured one swiftly.

He examined the spear. It was capably made of cut stone, crude but effective. The spear could not compete with the iron-tipped spears employed by his Zulu brethren, but the stone spear would suffice. Badoo's intention was to keep in reserve the Thompson sub-machine gun for his instincts had already warned him of a greater impending danger.

He waited and observed the stars. The constellations swept in an arc, and when the jungle was darkest, he initiated his plan. Accepting that some animals can learn behavior, he intended on instilling fear into the slovenly Uhaite. Most of the beast-men were sleeping, but one brute in particular was restless. Badoo tossed small pebbles at his prone form, which agitated him further. He was part of a group of men sleeping on the ground in a circle about the campfire. Eventually, he awoke, and rose to his feet.

The beast-man blinked, rubbing the sleep from his eyes, and squinted into the darkness. He ambled about trying to understand what had awakened him. Badoo hefted the spear and with a mighty throw, he catapulted the spear at the beast-man. The spear penetrated the man's chest, punched out of his back, gore dripping from the stone point. The beast-man froze in his tracks, his mouth open and his eyes wide. His hands twitched at his sides. His eyes rolled upward as a bloody foam erupted from his throat and splattered onto his lips. He fell sideways with a grunt, twitched for a few seconds, and lay still.

Badoo watched with curiosity but no other members of this evil tribe stirred or noticed what had transpired. They would find the body when they awoke, and wonder at the nature of this man's death. Badoo slipped away.

He slept with his back propped up against a tree, the Thompson at his side. He did not dream, but when he awoke, he was rested and in the morning fog, he saw vague but familiar shapes walking away from him, and the spirit world blended into the blue mist as the first rays of the sun cut across the jungle. He thought for a moment that he recognized his deceased father's silhouette, but when he blinked, his attention was drawn to the distant ululation of the Uhaite who had discovered their slain comrade.

Badoo wasted no time. Following our trail into the foothills, he soon encountered a second group of beast-men. This was the group that had attacked us on the cliffs, nearly impaling me with a spear. They never saw Badoo who quickly slipped into the eastern jungle and began a circuitous route toward the cliffside village.

Later, hearing the gunfire as we fought our way up the trail and clambered over the rocks at the village periphery, Badoo had traveled far enough east to make his participation impossible. He wasn't concerned about us, although the gunfire provided him a better sense of the village's location. In fact, Badoo had been aware for some time that the Chinese were infiltrating the jungle and he considered them far more dangerous than the beast-men.

Badoo heard the Chinese talking, and he went to great lengths to conceal himself. Ever the scientist, I inquired of him as to the description of the foliage that concealed him, and naturally, Badoo simply laughed.

Badoo is tall, so he must have hidden in a thick cluster of elephant fronds. He listened to the Chinese without understanding their language, Cantonese, but by listening he had a sense for their personalities. These were uneducated men, driven by greed, hired hands that enjoyed killing. They all carried rifles and smoked incessantly. All in in all, an unhealthy, evil group of men.

When he heard them firing at Rocco and me, Badoo followed the sound of gunfire, and within minutes, he had killed the small group of Chinese pirates that most certainly would have slain Rocco and I if not for his intervention and expertise with a Thompson sub-machine gun.

TEN

We emerged from the jungle an hour later. Rarahu studied Badoo with interest and I quickly filled him in on our close-shave. Badoo, in turn, informed us that the ship had been taken and that Edgar and Doc were now captives. Immediately, Rocco proposed that we counter-attack and kill all of the Chinese. Rarahu, however, encouraged restraint. He pointed at the western sky. A mountain of purple clouds had materialized in contrast to the warm sun that still bathed the verdant jungle. A major storm was brewing, and we had to take shelter.

Rarahu sent some of his men to retrieve the dead Chinese, stating that it was unholy to leave bodies to rot in the jungle. He also pointed out that the stench of rotting bodies could incite the Uhaite beast-men into violence. Once the bodies were gathered, Rarahu had them piled with deadfall branches and burned. The speed in which his men accomplished this was impressive. They burned the bodies at the edge of town, and a short while later Rarahu's scouts informed him that the Chinese had retreated to their ship.

The news of Edgar and Doc's captivity did not sit well with Dusty and Johnny. They joined Rocco in expressing an acute interest in decimating the Chinese pirates, burning their ship, and putting a curse on all their relatives.

Our debate was cut short by the first sprinkle of rain. I encouraged Lani and her father to follow Rarahu into the building after explaining I needed a bath. Naturally, there was no argument. After emerging from the jungle both Rocco and I were covered in grime and stank to high heaven. Badoo, also seeing the wisdom of a tropical shower, followed us into a secluded alley where we stripped down and let the sudden onslaught of rain wipe us clean. The rain came down hard, and quickly. It was a warm, tropical rain, but gathering in ferocity. The sky had turned black. Jagged bolts of lightning speared the mountains of clouds that towered above us like another world.

I twisted my shirt and scrubbed it in the onslaught, rubbing the mud and moss from the cotton. We dressed in our wet clothes, knowing that they would dry quickly enough in the tropical heat. We returned to the building we had originally entered where Lani, the professor and the others were eating at a table. The food was primarily fruits and nuts with some grainy bread. It was delicious. Coming close to death always increases my appetite.

Satina and Johnny sat together and I caught bits of their conversation. Johnny was impressed that she could speak English so well. In fact, most of the Sumtoans understood and could speak various English terms, although only Satina, Tehani and Rarahu could speak English fluently. King Vaea made no effort to speak any but his own language, relying on interpreters for informational exchanges. Tehani tended to Dusty with his broken arm and I witnessed in them the identical blossoming of admiration that I saw in Satina and Johnny.

Outside, the storm raged. The constant drumbeat of thunder was punctuated by the angry detonations of the surf on the rocks. The black clouds had destroyed the sun and turned the world into a purple and gray beast that slashed at the island with lightning bolts and endless sheets of stinging rain. The road outside became a rushing stream of ferocious water splashing down the sloping path.

The wind was furious. It brought with it a stench of oil and mildew and the fecund odor of ancient earth and sea. The world as we had seldom known it was visible to us; this was the primal earth at the moment of creation, a brawling and uncontrollable deity intent on having its way. My crew and I had survived many storms both at sea and in port, but this storm was altogether different. So we sat for a while and sometimes exchanged a few words, but as the storm raged on we mostly sat tight and waited. The Sumtoans, to their credit, appeared content to sit safely in their primitive but sturdy buildings.

Rarahu assured us that his men had reported that the surviving Chinese had retreated to their ship, and there were no other aggressors on the island. The disposition of the freighter's crew was unknown, but professor Kawena was convinced that Victoria Ransom was aboard that freighter. I agreed. According to the professor, Victoria had left him stranded with instructions for him to convince the Sumtoans to give up their treasure or face dire consequences. King Vaea, for his part, had conveyed that the gods had already decided all of our fates, and there was nothing to do but rest and to eat, which he did exceedingly well.

King Vaea and his wife Oleka, and their son Turoa, indulged in excessive eating, but they had the loyalty of all Sumtoans. Indeed, King Vaea and his people were all convinced that the gods had made plans for all of us, and their attitude was to take life on its own terms as each day occurred. Their noble perspective was one that I was soon to learn could not be shaken, as most good people are not easily swayed from their faith.

The dark afternoon blended into a blistering twilight of raging wind and slashing rain. During the long hours, I was conscious of a slight rumbling, which I initially mistook for thunder. Eventually, I deduced that the slight tremors I felt beneath my grass mat were the volcanic hiccups of an awakening labyrinthine force.

By the time the various couples had dispersed to their quarters, I waited for my crew knowing their characters firsthand. We had pending business. Rocco, Badoo, Johnny and Dusty joined me at the table in a room lit by a flickering hurricane lamp. We were alone. I saw the wavering flame in Rocco's eyes, compounded by an intensity that spelled trouble for anyone that might cross him. Rocco began.

"The witch has taken Doc and Edgar, captain, and that doesn't sit right with us. Just so you know; there won't be any fancy soiree for her when we find her."

They all held their stares, waiting for my response, and I could not have been prouder of these fine men at that moment. But I was still the captain, and the captain had to respond in the manner of all captains, which was to promote diplomacy first.

"She's never demonstrated a homicidal streak before," I began, "and while I agree her taking hostages is disturbing, we can't simply rush her men and start shooting."

"Yes we can. I'll remind you those Chinese apes would have had no problem killing us if they could have, and according to the professor she's behind all of this."

"I know, but Rarahu made it clear they deserted the island. We don't even know where they are."

Rocco ran a palm over his stubbly chin. "Those Chinese muscle-men will be back. You know it, and we know it."

"Remember when we were in New Guinea?" I reminded him. "Those headhunters had us surrounded and would have had our carcasses for dinner, but I said wait, and sure enough, one of the mangy little rats spoke enough English to understand a bribe."

"You bribed him by offering up six bottles of scotch, and that was the last of our scotch I might add, and the dumb shits drank themselves unconscious. Those Chinese blokes won't fall for a trick like that."

"All I'm saying is let's be open to all possibilities before we kill them."

That elicited a smile from Rocco's hardened features. And for the briefest of seconds the flames of anger burning behind his eyes were banked.

"I'm all for killing them," Dusty stated.

"No argument from me," Johnny agreed.

Badoo, observing and listening to all of this, simply smiled.

"Rarahu's men have reported the ship is secure, so we're lucky they didn't sink her. Once we get Doc and Edgar back we can set sail."

"I'm all for that, captain," Rocco said, "but there is the matter of extricating them safely. I also want to point out that Sumtoa's volcano is putting a constant wrinkle in the carpet, if you get my drift."

"A volcanic eruption could be dangerous depending on the extent of the eruption. I'm afraid we won't know until it happens."

"All the more reason to get the hell out of here," Johnny argued. "The constant rumblings are getting on my nerves."

"Captain, that girl Tehani seems to have taken to me." We looked at Dusty and for a moment his innocent features were quite endearing. Here we were talking about a goddamn volcanic eruption that could kill us all, and Dusty had his mind on a girl. Rocco had to contain himself from laughing.

"By the way, captain," Johnny interjected. "I've noticed the same thing about Satina. The girl seems to like me a great deal. Of course, I can't blame her."

"Jumping Jesus!" Rocco said as he burst out laughing. "You two clowns are getting tight britches at the wrong time! We've got a small army of Genghis Khans to fight and you're thinking about Valentine's Day!"

A peal of thunder dropped from the sky followed by a rumbling beneath our feet. In a flash our strategizing was ended as the reality of our circumstances intruded upon the scene. The rain continued all afternoon— an afternoon that was like the blackest of nights. The ceaseless patter of angry rain beat at the cliffside village with an unrelenting gusto, so that when it finally ceased the sudden silence took us all by surprise.

I followed my crew outside where we immediately joined Rarahu and his men in checking the perimeter. There were no signs of any Chinese pirates, but Rarahu sent out scouts in every direction to see if they might spot any ships. We went up to the ledge near the treasure cave where our view of the west was unimpeded, and to our surprise we saw nothing but a yellow horizon laced with purple clouds.

Without any impending and immediate danger, the Sumtoans emerged from their shelters and proceeded to go about the business of collecting the rainwater. To ensure they had a constantly supply of fresh water, the Sumtoans had devised a system of clay jar placement at strategic points around town. These jars were collected and brought inside. They had also learned from the visiting missionaries to boil their drinking water.

Rarahu told us, "This evening you're invited to a ceremony of thanks at the pool of stars. My men will remain behind and guard the town. Our women will be happy if you join us."

None of us was certain what to expect, but I advised my crew we would attend their ceremony as a sign of respect. There are many versions of Buddhism spread out across the tropics, and I have learned the best approach is to watch, to learn, and to act respectfully. That's easy enough for my men and me because of our experience, but I have heard too many tales of a white man's ignorance when it comes to religions other than his own. Meanwhile, I harbored an unspoken but nagging concern for the well-being of Edgar and Doc. I couldn't believe that Victoria Ransom would harm them, but I also knew that her greed for pretty things—like a chest of pirate treasure—knew no boundaries, and that concerned me.

I instructed Dusty, Johnny and Badoo to leave their firearms behind, while Rocco and I wore our .45 automatics in a huckleberry sling under our shirts. I never leave anything to chance. As it turns out, the ensuing evening was one of magical sensuality the likes of which I had never experienced before.

The procession to the pool of stars began just before midnight. We began our trek into the jungle, following the identical path that nearly resulted in Rocco and me meeting his Italian ancestors in the hereafter. The humidity had risen dramatically but a night breeze caressed us, and I was feeling somewhat relaxed in the way that men like us have that are always ready to kill an attacker.

The stone bowl on the pedestal was filled with rainwater. Rarahu,

Oleka and Turoa made several fires around the clearing, but away from the pedestal. We were instructed to stand to one side while King Vaea spoke earnestly on matters I will never fathom. He raised his hands to the heavens and spoke to the stars, which twinkled mysteriously in the lavender heavens. Then Rarahu instructed us to walk around the pedestal without touching it. As we did so I saw to my astonishment, the starry night reflected in the water as if it were a mirror. The scene was magical and unreal, made all the stranger by the fact that suddenly Satina, Tehani and Oleka removed their sarongs and tied them about their waists. Their golden, ample bodies were an enticement of slender forms and erotic beauty. Oddly, I wasn't embarrassed by their nakedness. A beautiful, bare-breasted woman in the tropics is such a breathtaking sight that I cannot adequately express my admiration.

We moved aside and stood transfixed. Satina, Tehani and Oleka commenced singing and dancing in circles around the pedestal. Professor Kawena and Lani observed all of this with equal astonishment. Some time passed before the singing and dancing concluded. King Vaea brought forth several large clay jugs painted with bright colors. They passed around cups and we all shared in drinking from the jugs. It tasted dark, like Guinness except thinner, and lighter on the tongue. There was a sweet aftertaste. Rocco eyed the drink suspiciously, and drank very little. I cannot claim the same distinction. Blame it on the tropics. The warm, night air and the beautiful naked women were perhaps too much for me. I drank greedily. Dusty and Johnny and professor Kawena also drank their fill. I saw Lani drinking, too, and gazing at me over the rim of her cup.

Badoo, I noticed, had blended into the darkness. This was his habit, to slip away as a kind of silent watchman, observing and learning. I cannot imagine now what he learned from observing us. I cannot say with any certainty what, if any, hallucinogenic properties may have been evident in our drinks. I only know that I was deeply affected.

The stars tilted in the heavens, and the ripe jungle was alive with a green phosphorescence. Every living thing, every palm frond and blade of grass, and every flower or tree and bush, were all revealed to me as a living energy, and the true nature of life was apparent to us all. Perhaps I am too much the scientist and not enough of a novelist to do this scene justice. I understood things before in a way that was new and exciting. This was not necessarily a knowledge that I had been denied, but rather a fresh insight into things I already knew.

Glancing about I saw the glow of mushrooms sprouting from the jungle soil. I sensed the deep, hot lava crawling inexorably toward the surface, and each small creature or bird was aglow with life as it scampered or flew in dizzying patterns to and fro. I drank from an endless cup. Rocco was gone, and I laughed loudly. I may have called his name, chiding him to return to our circle where the small campfires sent yellow shadows fleeing into the darkness.

The women began singing and dancing again, this time in a frenzy. Their eyes shone with carnal delight, or so it appeared to me. Soon, we were joined by other villagers, old and young alike. The cups were passed around and everyone drank deeply. Professor Kawena was engaged in a discussion with an attractive, middle-age Sumtoan woman, but eventually I lost sight of them as the flames crackled hotly and the singing women danced in unison to a language that, for the briefest of moments, I thought I might decipher.

I came to see the dancing and singing as a celebration, and then, in one startling moment as I passed the stone bowl and its water reflecting the stars, the illusion was shattered by a sudden ripple as a volcanic surge swept across the island. I may not have felt the volcanic rumble in my intoxicated state, but because I happened to be staring at the water in the stone bowl, I alone saw the universe bend, and a chill ran down my spine.

My fear didn't last. Pushing thoughts of volcanic eruptions from my mind, I gloried in the sight of these beautiful women dancing gracefully. I smelled flowers, and humus, and the cool stone pedestal, and the water glittering with galaxies. Someone touched my arm. I spun about, laughing, and there was Lani, a strange light in her eyes. She smiled. Her shirt had become unbuttoned, and her hair had been whipped by a sea breeze. She was all that was good on the earth, and I took her hands in mine.

She spoke to me, but I can't recall her words. She told me later I spoke as well, but she only pretended to understand me. We were all speaking an ancient language, possessed in a way, by the ancient race that once inhabited all of this world, and whose spirits now linger only on those distant tropical islands.

It was a beautiful madness, perhaps, and possibly it was all real. It certainly still feels real to me now. There was laughter, dancing, and the maddening stars shimmering in a pool of water; so fragile was this world that I mourned its destruction even as I reveled in excess. Perhaps I am too much the scientist, and not enough of a novelist. The heavens blossomed with a clarity that the average person cannot see because their vision is clouded by neon and electricity.

I was suddenly aware of the great stretch of time and of this ancient earth. Not simply the tropical islands, but of all the earth and the elements of earth, air, fire and water all congealing by an unseen hand, fashioned in the tumultuous roar of eternity. Mankind was swimming in the light of multiple realities; one of their own making that included the sweltering concrete confines of civilization, and another world of a land rising from the mist of an antediluvian plain; a place of gods whose names are forgotten. A place where our past is resplendent with winged scavengers, wild beasts and roaming tribes of half-men, and ancient cities hidden now beneath the waves of this uncaring sea.

The unwritten history of mankind is one of lost civilizations and centuries of war and fear and survival, all whispered to us on a sea-breeze: I experienced an all too brief glimpse of another time witnessed from the stars and uncharted like Atlantis.

I felt the presence of the Great Creator, the one Creator that is linked to all religions, God, who goes by many names. I understood, too, that mankind is greedy and selfish, and men have forgotten the importance of their own souls. They allow themselves to be dictated to by the false purveyors of this or that organization, and in so doing their spirits have fled their bodies.

Lani's hand was soft and warm and I don't believe I let go of her hand for a very long time. We understood each other's primal, instinctive nature as we looked into each other's eyes. It was natural for her to remove her clothing, and we stepped aside, deeper into a fragrant jungle path out of sight of our comrades. Her golden skin was hot and sent a shudder of desire through me. I was holding her in my arms, her body pressed tightly to mine, when at last my lips found hers.

ELEVEN

I awoke beneath a blanket of ferns and elephant leaves. Lani was still sleeping gently in my arms. I was vaguely surprised when I opened my eyes that I didn't suffer from the outrageous hangover I'd been expecting. Quite the contrary, I was alert and felt rested and strong. What did disturb me was the sunlight streaming down on us. We had slept much longer than I intended, and while the morning was still fresh, the sun's elevation was several degrees higher than I preferred. I had intended to be awake before the sun rose.

...her body pressed tightly to mine...

I pulled on my clothes, and then glanced at Lani's breathtaking form. Such an image could never be painted so well even by the Renaissance masters. I felt an immediate desire to protect her from any harm, and that meant getting her off this island. I nudged her awake.

"Elliot." Hearing her speak my name was like listening to music.

"We slept too long."

Lani put her hand on my chest, a reassuring gesture. "It'll be all right."

She dressed and we hiked back to the clearing. The pool of stars was now a pool for several brightly colored small birds that were drinking the water. The sky was a rich texture of blue. When we reached the village, Rarahu met us.

"My men have seen the ships far out at sea. They are returning, and we will be ready. You will find your men inside."

Rocco was at a table stuffing some of the bread into his mouth. Dusty and Johnny had already eaten. None of us spoke about the things we experienced at the pool of stars.

"Where's Badoo?" I asked.

"He's gone to reconnoiter," Johnny said, "and he told us to tell you that each man follows his own destiny, and that the omens today are both good and bad."

"Mumbo jumbo," Rocco said.

"We're going to the ship," I announced, "and once on board we'll clear the lagoon and radio the Australian or British outposts, whichever picks up the signal. We'll attack the pirates and get Edgar and Doc home as soon as we have an opportunity."

"There's one thing, captain," Dusty interjected. "Tehani is going with us. King Vaea pronounced us man and wife last night."

"Cap'n, I married Satina last night as well," Johnny added.

"It's true, captain," Rocco said. "Good old King Vaea was having himself a happy time last night, and then he went and married off these two with Rarahu translating. *The Reaper's Scythe* is now set for a honeymoon cruise."

Somehow I wasn't surprised, although I should have been. So much had happened to us in such a short period of time that being surprised just wasn't possible for me.

"All right. All the more reason to keep Edgar busy cooking, but our first priority is to save our shipmates."

Dusty grinned. "I'm looking forward to Edgar's stew. This diet of fruit, bread and coconuts is fine, but I've got a hankerin' for more. I told Tehani his stew will fatten her up!"

Rarahu had made preparations to repel a second attack, but I thought we stood a better chance if we could secure our ship. We had extra guns and ammunition on board, and I doubted if they bothered to remove it. Greed has a tendency to blind men—and women - and cloud their judgment.

I asked Rarahu to speak with King Vaea about evacuating the island. Professor Kawena had joined us to state his growing fear that the volcano was about to erupt. To our great sadness, King Vaea rejected all talk of evacuating his people. Nor would he except any assistance from the Australian authorities. The Sumtoan people were steadfast in their belief that their god (or was it *gods*?) had decided their destiny and they did not fear death. Other than the newlyweds, Satina and Tehani, he only allowed his son Turoa to accompany us, but Turoa insisted on staying with his people.

We were preparing our trek down into the valley and back to our ship when one of Rarahu's men reported that the pirates had returned and were being led by "the evil woman" that had stranded professor Kawena here months ago. I had no doubt as to who he meant by "evil woman" and we ventured downslope to await her arrival.

I spied them through the binoculars, initially struck by the fact that I discerned no sign of the Uhaite, the beast-men. This struck me as unsettling. Their absence led me to believe that the cogs of a great orchestrated activity were being manipulated unseen by us, and the result would be dangerous. I said as such to Rocco.

"If anyone could control those beast-men it would be Victoria," he said, "but that's stretching the boundaries of possibility."

"Those beastsies have disappeared since the Chinese showed up, and I don't believe they're afraid of anyone."

"So the beasty-boys and the Chinese are allies in some way."

"And they'll come at us from two directions, or three directions."

"That'll do it," Rocco nodded.

We knew that the odds we faced were insurmountable, and that there was a great likelihood that some of us would be killed or seriously injured. At the heart of this fact lie the thought that greed had driven Victoria Ransom to this point. But how far would she go? I couldn't answer that question. Greed is something that works on a person in the same manner as a disease. Victoria was greedy, and after seeing the treasure cave, I knew she would go to great lengths to secure that treasure.

My initial thought was to reason with her, bargain for a portion of the treasure in exchange for safe passage for my crew, and as many of the Sumtoans that wished to join us. Once free of the island, I would dispatch an emergency radio SOS about the impending volcanic eruption.

As it turned out, we would have little time to plan for anything. Rarahu's men had come back to report the arrival of a large party led by a woman. They were approaching through the same valley that we had traversed. We waited by the ledge where I had so recently avoided being impaled. Rarahu had men with rifles hidden in the jungle. Badoo had yet to reappear, but I wasn't concerned about him. The professor, Lani, Rocco, Dusty, Johnny and Rarahu and I all waited as her troop marched leisurely up the trail, including far too many Chinese brutes. There was still no sign of the beast-men. Tension hung in the air like an invisible weight.

I saw her in the distance, a bright flash of pink amongst the green ferns and yellow flowers. She was wearing a pink shirt tied off above her belly-button, the sleeves short, and her buttons loose so that her cleavage was visible. Her auburn hair touched her shoulders lightly, the curls catching the sun. A pistol resided in a hip holster like an accessory chosen from a movie studio's prop department. Her knee-high boots were freshly polished, the tight cut of her khaki trousers firm against her muscled legs. She reminded me of some fashion model from a magazine advertisement, beautiful but somehow haughty and distant.

As I scanned the troop with the binoculars, I came upon a sight that disturbed me greatly. Far back amongst her men stood a giant. He must have been six and a half feet tall, his broad tattooed shoulders gleaming with perspiration. He was shirtless, and his chest and arms were immense. I had never seen a man that tall and the Chinese were not known for their height. This man was an oddity, his muscles bulging on his arms like living things, the veins jutting out like worms crawling beneath his skin.

As they moved closer I saw that his legs, in fact, were not long, rather, his height came from his abnormally shaped torso, his arms longer than his legs. He was yet another oddity of nature; a man dealt a genetic deck of cards at birth that was the one in a million difference in the gene pool. He was bald, with a small mouth, fat nose, his eyes close together as if they had been stitched onto his face. He moved slower than the others because of his short legs, which must have struggled to keep up with all of that weight pressing down on his knees. The sweat dripped from him, his face a scowl of displeasure. I knew instantly that this giant was Victoria's secret weapon.

I also spotted Thad Bellamy in the group, one of Victoria's "business associates" for many years, and a man that I not only disliked, but a man that I felt had no moral fiber in his soul at all. Bellamy had worked for Victoria for many years, and I never trusted him. He stood about five feet eleven inches and the shape of his head and his nose reminded me of a rodent perpetually sniffing around for scraps.

I handed the binoculars to Rocco. Rocco watched the procession for a moment and handed the binoculars back to me.

"They'll be close enough in a moment. She has Edgar and Doc with her."

I saw them now, down the trail and just behind Victoria. They were not shackled at all and walking freely, although both men looked out of sorts. I could well imagine the peace of mind they offered Victoria at being taken from the ship. Another few minutes passed and Victoria had come up closer, looking my way with interest. When they were down below us, just twenty-five feet away, she stopped and the procession stopped with her.

Victoria took her time removing a blue silk bandanna from her pocket and wiping the sweat from her face.

"Hello Elliot," she said, looking up at me. "I admit to being excited when we saw your ship anchored in the bay. You always had a nose for trouble; I'll grant you that. Just so that there is no misunderstanding, the treasure is mine, all of it. I might grant you a trinket or two for old time's sake, but that does depend on your behavior."

She was accompanied by Thad Bellamy, who hung back, and two imposing pirates. One was the ugly giant I had seen, and the other was the Fu Manchu character with the snake tattoos on his forearms. They stared at me without blinking.

"Send Doc and Edgar up. My men will help them climb over the ledge."

Victoria raised a manicured eyebrow. "Of course. It was my pleasure to have them as guests. That bay, as you know, is home to a rather hungry Kraken. In fact, my Chinese friends have come with .50 caliber guns mounted on their ship to dissuade the creature from getting frisky."

The corners of her mouth turned up in a half smile. Doc and Edgar began their ascent and Johnny and Rocco helped pull them over the ledge. Doc, grunting and cursing, offered a few colorful remarks in Victoria's direction, which she ignored. I greeted both of them and returned my attention to our beautiful problem.

"That treasure belongs to King Vaea and the Sumtoan people," I declared.

"Elliot, by now you know the volcanic activity has increased. King Vaea is happy enough with his darling young wife. The treasure belongs to me. Professor Joseph Kawena was instructed to explain the facts of life to these lovely, albeit backwards people. I have no time for discussion, and there will be no negotiating. A lava flow could seal that cave forever. You have one hour."

At this, she turned and spoke a few words in Cantonese at which point the giant brute came lumbering forward. She locked her gaze on mine, and that's when I saw it. That was when I knew Victoria had gone too far; I knew that she was consumed by her own selfish desires. It flickered in her eyes like a dark flame, and emanated from her body like an evil aura. I could feel it.

"His name is Dae Hang Maau, which roughly translates as deprived giant. You have no idea what it took for me to control him. In the end, it was his common desire for sex. I have contracted with the tallest and stoutest prostitutes from Hong Kong to please him. Three at once usually does it. Of course, he still had to be trained. He killed the first one. In his excitement, he accidentally strangled her. It cost me a pretty penny to keep the Hong Kong authorities from looking into the matter."

"Let me shoot them both now!" Rocco rasped next to me.

"Naturally, Dae Hang Maau is supported by the descendants of the fabled Zheng Shi, the lady pirate of China" she continued. "No doubt you've seen how well-armed they are. Elliot, you're outnumbered."

"I've been outnumbered before," I retorted, trying to sound braver than I felt. "You're the one that needs to reconsider, Victoria. There is no way I'll let you take the treasure and harm any of these people."

"Allow me to introduce you to another of my associates," she said, half turning and gesturing to the pirate with the snake tattoos writhing on his forearms. His Fu Manchu mustache glistened with sweat. "This is Zhang Chen. He's the leader of these men. He doesn't like getting his hands dirty, so he pays his men very well. He has a talent for watching and learning. He's been watching you and he actually believes you are a formidable opponent." She gave a little giggle, which sounded innocuous. "It was Zhang Chen here who recommended Dae Hang Maau as a means of putting you in your place. I'm not taking any chances, Elliot."

"You had no way of knowing I was even here."

"We had followed the professor's daughter. Word of a beautiful woman traveling alone never goes unnoticed in this part of the world. I knew who she was immediately, so we kept an eye on her. We had you spotted in Singapore, Elliot, and since we were coming here anyway, we followed you."

"There's no reason to take this any further. King Vaea and the Sumtoan people have done nothing wrong. This is their home, and you…"

"Enough!" Victoria raised her hand. "I am going to have that treasure or

Zhang Chen's men will attack. You should know me well enough by now. I am not to be crossed. I always get what I want."

"This island is too crowded," I countered, trying to sound flippant. "Why don't you just go home?"

I felt Zhang Chen's eyes burning a hole in me. It was unnerving.

"You have one hour."

She turned her back on me, and I felt her disdain hit me like a wave.

I immediately conferred with Doc and Edgar as to their numbers.

"What you see is it, except for a small crew left aboard the ship. Those men aren't fighters. They were hired to operate the freighter. There are also a few Chinese aboard the pirate ship."

"Her cook is an idiot," Edgar offered. "Everything he cooks has rice in it."

"They were upset by the failure of her men to take the town," Doc continued. "We heard they lost a few men and I knew it was you and Rocco."

Rocco and I had started counting heads. She had twenty-eight men with her, including Dae Hang Maau and his stumpy legs and over-sized arms.

Victoria and her crew had backed up, setting up a temporary camp just out of sight down the trail. I turned around and Professor Kawena and Lani were staring at me. The look on their faces spoke volumes. They were frightened, and they expected us to save them.

I instructed Lani and her father to remain inside until the attack was over. Once again I found myself trying to sound confident. Rarahu had stationed his riflemen in strategic places out of view. I looked around and didn't see them, but I knew they were there. Turoa had joined Rarahu and both appeared unconcerned. This was their standard attitude. No matter how bad things got, they remained calm and ready to fight.

The first wave of the attack happened swiftly.

TWELVE

Dusty and Johnny remained in the village. Edgar and Doc wanted to join the fight, but I ordered to them remain inside with Lani and her father. They didn't like it, but both men were too exhausted to be of much help.

Rocco and I slipped over the ledge and went down the trail after Victoria, but we cut into the jungle before we saw them. We heard voices on the trail and the crackling underbrush that meant the jungle was occupied by men once again. The last thing I wanted was another jungle fight. We heard gunfire in the distance. It came from town, behind us, and it meant that Dusty and Johnny were already busy.

Rocco and I ventured down an incline some fifteen feet from the trail that led up to the village. I saw a man nearby with his back to us. He was urinating against a tree. Rocco snuck up behind him and slit his throat.

We proceeded cautiously. The jungle was alive with a flurry of sounds.

A sudden shudder tilted us sideways, and a massive explosion shook the trees. At first, I thought that the Chinese had let loose with some type of cannon or had used explosive, but then the awful truth dawned on us.

The volcano had begun to erupt.

A plume of black smoke had whipped skyward, blossoming into a black mountain. Rocco cursed. We couldn't see the volcano tip from this vantage point, but the smoke and the subsequent peripheral explosions told the tale.

We burst out of the jungle onto the trail and swerved right. We should have emerged at the spot where Victoria had pitched camp, but to our amazement, they were gone. Everything was gone. Their equipment, tents, and all of those angry-looking Chinese pirates, had vanished.

The volcanic shudders had agitated the wildlife. The air was alive with screeching bird sounds, and the greenery was bristling with activity. We made our way down the rocky path wary of an ambush, but nothing happened.

I estimated we were a half mile from the ledge that led up to the village, a modest distance under normal circumstances. Rocco and I never spoke, bur because we are of like minds, we turned simultaneously and headed toward the village. We had been gone a solid thirty minutes and accomplished nothing. All the more disturbing was the fact that we felt as if somehow we had been duped. I wracked my mind for a plausible method for Victoria and her minions to breach the town's perimeter, but I came up blank.

We hustled up the ridge and clambered toward the village. We were greeted with pandemonium. Rarahu's riflemen were firing into that section of jungle that cut below the volcanic hills. The rifle fire was steady. Rarahu himself greeted us with his usual calm demeanor. Further up near the treasure cave we heard the steady crack of gunfire as well.

"They scaled the cliff near the cave," Rarahu explained. "It must have taken them all night. They have men in the jungle, but we can hold them. Our danger comes from the cliffside."

The first thing I did was check on Lani and the professor. They were inside one of smaller buildings. Dusty was their guard, and Satina, Tehani, Oleka and some older women were with them. To his credit, the professor volunteered to grab a gun and fight, but I talked him out of it. To make him feel better, Dusty gave him a revolver, and this visibly pleased the professor.

Rocco had gone up the incline toward the treasure cave. Some of the Chinese had successfully infiltrated the town and had slipped into the rocky escarpments that bordered the hilly plateau behind the treasure cave. The boulders and ledges here were sharp and nearly impossible to climb, at least at a glance. However, the Chinese had demonstrated great skill and somehow positioned themselves in the rocks. They could not have done this without great effort and danger to themselves. As proof of this, the mangled body of a Chinese pirate lay upon a lower boulder after slipping from one of the cliffs during their nighttime climb.

Our one advantage here lay in the fact that the pirates could not come down from their positions without being picked off. Yet this fact was still not comforting. Rocco and I decided that if we might increase our odds a bit by plugging away at these mangy boulder rats.

As Rocco examined the sweeping rocks above us, I concentrated on a nearby combatant who occasionally peeked out to growl at us. His position wasn't good, so I winged a .45 shot at him, knowing I'd miss. Remarkably, the slug must have ricocheted off the boulder and winged him. I heard him yelp in pain, followed by a slinging cacophony of Cantonese insults.

Rocco was staring intently to his left, upslope, but I couldn't see any pirates. "I see a glint of something, and its moving downhill. One of the buggers is trying to sneak up on us. I'll be right back."

Rocco vanished between two boulders, and a few minutes later I heard the solitary crack of a .45 automatic. A few moments later Rocco re-appeared. "Got him."

"Let's move inside these cliff trails and see if we can see something other than the occasional cowlick," I suggested.

We paused to reconnoiter thirty feet along a rocky cliff. Above us, the ridges narrowed between several mounds of volcanic rock. We could hear the pirates scampering about, but we couldn't see them. The thought crossed my mind that I had come up with this foolish idea to attack the pirates when we should have been making our retreat. I said so to Rocco, but that dark gleam in his eye told me the blood-lust was on him. Another trembling wave from the volcano reinforced my desire to get back to the ship. We might have engaged in a brief debate on the topic when a voice behind us caused us to stop. We slowly turned around.

"Easy with the guns, boys," Victoria said, stepping out from behind a boulder, "and keep your hands high. What a sight you two make!" She had a revolver in her hand.

She also had the giant Dae Hang Maau with her, Zhang Chen, and two other pirates with rifles leveled on us. No sooner had I set my gaze on Victoria than Rocco dashed around a corner firing his .45, but missing. Instantly the two riflemen opened up, their bullets shattering into the rocks where Rocco had been standing. Stone chips and dust whipped into my face. Rocco had disappeared and Victoria began screaming.

"Damn your eyes, Elliot! If you move they'll shoot you down!"

"Let me get some of these people off the island," I pleaded. I hated the fact that Zhang Chen stared at me impassively. He never spoke, and he never changed his expression.

"Put your gun down!"

I had raised my hands with the .45 pointing skyward, and I could have shot her then as I lowered them, but the two Chinese had their rifles trained on my head. I crouched and slowly set the Colt on the ground. I didn't like the look in Victoria's eyes. I knew this woman well, very well indeed, but what I saw at that moment was unnerving. It wasn't merely larceny and greed that I saw in those once bright eyes, but a stygian flare that spoke of her murderous intent. She had been consumed in some way since I had last seen her; and while her exterior remained that of a beautiful woman, I saw now the horrific distillation of evil that had devoured her soul.

"Let me get some of these people off the island," I repeated. "They're innocent. Is all this treasure worth what you're doing?"

Her perfect lips turned up in a snarl. "Oh yes, Elliot, it's worth it. That treasure is one of a kind. Don't you understand? It is the greatest single treasure in the history of mankind, and it's all right here under your very nose! Don't be such a bleeding heart for these backwater natives." She paused, her gaze ripping holes in me. "We had something once, you and I, and it was fun for a little while. But you spend too much time photographing sea shells and sand crabs. How droll you've become! But I'll do you one final favor, Elliot, I'll give you a sporting chance."

She turned and barked something in Cantonese, and the two riflemen went after Rocco. Then she looked up at Dae Hang Maau who had been watching me silently the entire time. When she spoke to him he grunted, and it sounded for the world like the grunt of a hungry animal. Victoria picked up my gun and stuck it in her belt. She wriggled her revolver at me.

"Dae Hang Maau loves to fight. As you can see, he doesn't have a gun. I promised him three harlots if he kills you. He's all yours, Elliot." She gave a little laugh, and with a haughty twist of her hips, Victoria and Zhang Chen turned around and walked away before I could say another word. Zhang Chen might have had the beginning of a smile on his lips.

Dae Hang Maau was smiling, too. I didn't like that smile.

He bent over and picked up a branch that had blown onto the rocks during the storm. It was a big branch, but it looked small in his hands. There were no branches for me to use as a club.

He started forward and I slipped inside his reach and slammed a fist into his gut. I had hoped to double him over, but the punch had little effect. I moved back, trying to circle him. He was cumbersome, slow, top-heavy. I thought I might slip past him but he was onto that idea. His enormous frame blocked my way. There was no way I could slip past him unless I took him down.

He struck me swiftly with the branch. I had no idea his could move his arms that fast. The blow knocked what breath remained from my lungs. I wheezed, fighting for breath, and backed up before he could hit me again.

He lumbered toward me. I set myself in a crouch, waiting for him to move in. When he was close enough, I kicked upwards, aiming for his groin, hoping to use my kick like a battering ram at his one vulnerable spot. He jolted backwards, dazed for just an instant, grunting in pain. It wasn't enough. Before I could regain my balance and strike again, he swung a hammy fist that nailed me on the side of the head, sending me sprawling.

I desperately kicked again, and I struck his knee. He didn't falter, but I saw the pain in his eyes. So his knees were weak, too. I kicked him again, and again, both times on the same knee. That hurt him. He wobbled, saliva dripping from his sneering, lower lip, and I grabbed the club and twisted it quickly from his hands.

I hit him with the club as hard as I could. The wood caught him on the left side of the head. I thought I had him, because, for a second, his eyes seemed to roll up in their sockets, but he shook his head and righted himself. With a bellow, he grabbed me and held me in a bear hug. He lifted me off my feet, squeezing hard. His biceps were like steel. The breath began to leave my lungs. Black spots were swimming before my eyes. Somehow,

I got my arms free and I managed to reach up and put my thumbs in his eyes. That was a mistake. He roared with anger and pain and shook me the way an animal shakes a carcass after the kill. Except I wasn't dead, not yet.

I dug my thumbs in, and he let go. I dropped like a sack of grain to the ground and rolled out of his reach. He was bellowing in pain and rage, lashing out with his hands trying to grab me. Tears pooled in his eyes, clouding his vision. I had slowed him down but I still hadn't stopped him. When I lost my footing trying to dodge his arms, he managed to grab me and he tossed me against the rocks as if I were a rag-doll.

He would have had me then if he wasn't handicapped by those short legs. I jumped to my feet, backing away, my breath coming in hard rasps through my exhausted lungs. I crawled away like a beaten dog.

I was too tired to get to my feet. I craned my neck around and watched him turning, muttering some Cantonese gibberish. I waited for him to come closer. He had one weakness and exploiting that weakness was my only chance.

I waited until he was nearly on top of me. Then I swung my feet around and slammed them against his leg while I grabbed his dangling wrist. He howled in pain, and using his arm, I pulled myself up and spun away before he could think about grabbing me.

I stood facing him, unsure of what to do next. I saw no way that I could beat him, and he seemed to know it. He gestured for me to come forward. I didn't know what he was saying, but I could guess.

Come on! You can't win! I'll kill you quick!

I was impossibly slow; a weakling compared to this giant.

I circled him again, but I could never get him in position where I could sprint past and break for freedom. He was canny, positioning his body in such a way where I couldn't dash onto the open trail. Escape was my only option now. I was doomed unless I might get my hands on a knife or gun.

Since I couldn't get past him, I realized I had no choice but to flee in the other direction, following Rocco up into the volcanic boulders. I didn't favor that idea either, but if I could find Rocco we had a chance to kill Dae Hang Maau with Rocco's gun.

This turned out be a foolhardy move. I had climbed some fifty feet on a winding path when I came under fire from the Chinese higher up in the rocks. I could hear Dae Hang Maau shuffling in my direction, grunting from the exertion of carrying his bulky body up such a steep incline.

When he finally turned the corner and saw me he was breathing heavily, but he still managed to smile. It was not a pretty smile. His yellow, cracked

...he tossed me against the rocks...

teeth and the dark maw of cavities made his leer into something obscene. I felt like a specimen about to be consumed by a monster.

I picked up a hefty rock. There were several other large rocks strewn about. Before he had time to think, I threw the rock at his head with all of my strength. The rock struck him above his left eye and split open his skin. It was a deep cut, and blood poured freely from the wound. He bellowed in rage and pain.

I took advantage of the moment by sprinting forward throwing a flurry of punches at his body. There was nothing behind my punches, and his body was too thick for me to do any damage. The sonofabitch was as solid as a brick wall. I had to be careful not to let him grab onto me. He appeared fearless. I kicked him again in his left knee, fast and hard. He moved back quickly. I hadn't done any damage but the pain was getting to him.

I picked up another rock. I knew he was going to kill me, and I was resigned to it. But I intended on hurting him before I died. This rock had a sharp point to it. I brought my arm back and pretended to throw the rock to gauge his reaction. He was able to bring his arms up in a defensive posture, and lean a little to his right. He looked perplexed to see that I hadn't thrown the rock after all.

I repeated the maneuver, swinging my arm quickly, but holding onto the rock. His actions were identical, and he had stopped his forward motion. He didn't like the rocks. His arms came up; he cringed and moved his upper torso. It wasn't exactly an impasse, but I had a moment to think. I had hurt the bastard. I needed to hurt the bastard some more.

We looked at each other. I darted forward, kicking low at his legs, and then I heaved the sharp rock at his head. The rock cut into his right cheek, tearing a gash in the flesh. He bellowed some more, swinging his arms and trying to hit me. The rock had fallen near me and I picked it up gain.

Dae Hang Maau's face was bloody from the two wounds. He made no effort to stanch the blood flow. The blood dripped down his face and onto his shirt. It wasn't enough to slow him down, and all I had accomplished was to make him angrier. I kept kicking at his knees and legs, connecting several times. It was useless, and I knew it. I was tired, but I had made him bleed. It was a small victory.

I heaved the rock again, and this time the point struck him in the eye. He screamed in agony, both hands sweeping up to his head. I thought I had my chance to slip past him so I crouched and ran around his left side, but he must have sensed what I was doing. His arm came down with a greater speed than I anticipated he struck me a mighty blow. I went crashing to the ground, dazed.

Still bellowing, he held his left hand up to his injured left eye, and with his right hand he grabbed my ankle. He lifted me with one arm as if I were weightless. The breath had been knocked out me, and suddenly I was looking at the trail upside-down. I tried to twist free, but his grip on my ankle was like iron. We remained in that position for a moment, with him grunting in pain and holding his bloody eye, all while I was held upside-down. I was stunned, and I knew I was finished.

That was when I saw Rocco from my upside-down position, looking astonished as he came racing out from behind a boulder. He raised his .45 automatic and shot Dae Hang Maau in the head. I felt the hot splash of brain and blood that burst from his skull like a melon shattering after being dropped from a great height, and his body slumped backward. Even in death the vicious giant still held onto my ankle as I lay there trying to catch my breath.

THIRTEEN

"I can't wait to tell the boys in the Sydney pubs all about this," Rocco was saying. "Upside-down you were, dangling like a kewpie doll."

My ankle felt swollen, and every muscle in my body was protesting my exertions. I wanted a shot of whiskey and a bunk to sleep in.

"Victoria took my gun," was all I managed to say.

"It's time we went after her, Cap'n. I say we go after her the way a dog sniffs out a rat, tear the bitch to pieces, and get off this island."

I agreed. Victoria had played us for fools every step of the way. We were past negotiating. I wanted to get my hands around her lovely neck myself and choke her to death the way that Dae Hang Maau had wanted to choke me.

We retreated, and I was mostly limping as we departed from the hillside. A few shots were sent our way by the Chinese pirates, but after my encounter with Dae Hang Maau they seemed like irritating mosquitos. I was content to leave them in the hills and seek out their boss.

To our surprise, there was scant activity in the village. Dusty and Johnny reported that they had repelled the attack, and there was no sign of any pirates, Victoria or her cronies. The rumblings beneath the surface had subsided as well, and while we never mentioned it, we all knew this was a temporary recess. We needed to get off the island, and when I looked at Lani, I felt again a sense of urgency. I would do anything to protect her.

It was mid-day, and with plenty of daylight remaining, I was determined to find a resolution. Rocco was quick to remind me the only resolution that we should consider was in killing them all. Frankly, if we had more men I would have done just that, but we were still outnumbered. We were also boxed in. We soon learned that Victoria had stationed her men down that winding path leading to the village. With the pirates and their rifles in the adjacent hills, we had nowhere to go. I armed myself with an extra .45 from the backpack and stuffed the last of our loaded clips into my vest pockets.

During this lull, I was approached by Lani. She set her hand gently on my arm and looked up at me. "Elliot, I need you to be honest with me. What chance do we really have? Is there a way we can get to the ship?"

I wanted to lie to her, and I wanted to reassure her that everything was going to be fine, but I knew she would sense the lie. Still, I couldn't give up hope, and I wasn't one to surrender, and neither would my crew.

"We're in a tight spot," I said, "but as long as we're breathing we have a chance. I'm not giving up. Tell your father to be ready to go at a moment's notice. As soon as the opportunity presents itself we're going to the ship."

Nevertheless, we had nothing to do but wait, and waiting was torturous as the earth shook beneath our feet and a steady tendril of acrid smoke snaked from the volcano, dispersing on the breeze like specters suddenly freed from hades.

Late that afternoon, voices called to us downhill, and we watched from the cliff as Thad Bellamy came into view. He had a white handkerchief tied to a stick. He called out to us. "It's a truce!"

I never liked Bellamy, and I never bothered to get to know him. He was a businessman and friend of Victoria's, and I suspected they had a romantic involvement. His presence on Sumtoa was evidence enough that they had a stronger connection as I had previously suspected.

"Why shouldn't we shoot you now, Bellamy?" I called down to him.

"Listen, Elliot, Victoria knows that you defeated Dae Hang Maau. We found the body. Congratulations, we are all quite impressed. He must have been quite a handful."

"Get on with it," I said. "You didn't come here to flatter me."

"No, no of course not. Elliot, all we want is that treasure. You need to listen to reason. You're surrounded, but you can have your ship. Sure, it's fine if you take a little treasure for yourself. Really, that's fine, but leave now and we won't interfere."

"I don't trust you or Victoria," I replied flatly.

"What choice do you have? We have superior firepower, and we have the men. Zhang Chen is prepared to order a full-scale attack. He's been telling Victoria that you are dangerous and that you have to die. Defeating the big Chinaman was impressive, but he says you've gotta go, Elliot."

There was no question in my mind that the odds were against us. I also knew that Victoria did not intend to let us reach our ship, but we had no choice. The Victoria I had known had been consumed by her own greed.

"Give us a minute."

Rocco leaned in and said, "We should accept, and then when they make their move we kill them."

"Except we don't know when they'll make their move."

"Once Victoria has the treasure there won't be any need for her to pretend about anything."

"We can't give them the treasure."

"We won't, but we'll let them think they can have it."

"King Vaea will have to agree to that. We need to stall for time and come up with a better plan."

I turned back to Bellamy and yelled, "Thirty minutes!"

Fate would intervene, however, and any plans being made by either group were negated by the sudden volcanic explosion that shook the island. It sent a lava rain down into the jungle. The earth beneath us shuddered and a deep, rumbling sound was followed by an explosive sound. We were all jarred and nearly knocked off our feet.

Part of the mountainside had experienced what they call a non-explosive effusive eruption and released a steady stream of lava that began pouring out of the cliff-side like withering, molten serpents. Smoke and steam hissed to life, rippling upward, the after-shocks a constant reminder that this volcanic heap sat atop an angry monster. In addition to the eruption, an explosion had occurred further away; presumably on the other side of the volcano. We all heard it and felt it.

I glanced down the trail again and Bellamy was gone. No surprise there; the man was born a coward. Meanwhile, we were alarmed by both the eruption and the ground-shaking after-shocks.

Rocco and I joined up with Professor Kawena, Rarahu, Turoa, and the rest of my crew. I instructed Johnny and Dusty to prepare to evacuate and head for the ship. They immediately began helping Satina and Tehani in gathering their personal belongings. I asked Lani to assist them.

Professor Kawena took the opportunity to enlighten us as to the volcanic eruptions. He was convinced the island was going to experience a larger eruption, but estimating the correct time frame was impossible. Explosive eruptions are far more devastating than effusive eruptions, and Sumtoa had experienced both. Such preliminary eruptions often foreshadow an explosive eruption wherein the volcano spews volcanic ash and smoke, while the explosion itself destroys the landmass surrounding the volcano. This is what happened on Krakatoa in1883.

I'd had enough, and it was time to go. I informed Rarahu and Turoa to tell King Vaea one final time that we advised evacuation. I stood and gazed down the trail where Bellamy had disappeared, and where presumably Victoria and her Chinese apes were still camped.

"Captain, Badoo is either dead or up to something." Rocco said, interrupting my reverie.

"He's not dead, and whatever he's up to spells trouble for Victoria."

"I wish he'd at least send us a sign."

"That's not his way. He'll find us when he can."

Rarahu and Turoa had organized some men to gather the Zebu from the grassy hidden valley and get them out of harm's way. The molten lava was creeping through the jungle at an alarming rate, and within hours it would threaten to breach the valley. We hustled into the jungle and marked the lava's progress. At its widest, the lava flow was sixteen feet across, and slithering like some primeval snake, a plump and sizzling creature all fiery and unrelenting. Nature at times is fearsome, awe-inspiring, and decidedly lethal.

King Vaea emerged from one of the buildings accompanied by Oleka. He gestured to us, and Rarahu spent a few minutes listening to him. I detected nothing urgent in his tone, but he spoke at great length, and Rarahu listened intently. Finally, he turned to us and delivered King Vaea's message.

"It is the King's wish that we should conquer this evil woman and her men, and as payment for this you may fill a bag of whatever treasure can fit into this sack." Oleka handed me a folded burlap sack, which once unfolded, could easily hold a mighty treasure.

"You will choose your treasure now," Rarahu continued, "because the gods have chosen that such treasure is a temptation to evil men and women, and the serpent's hot breath will seal the treasure cave soon. We have given ourselves to this land and will return to the land."

Rarahu paused. "It's difficult to explain. The King has his own religious ideas that come from many sources. I cannot say this in English to do it justice. He said that Jo Jo, the professor, is an instrument of the gods, and that he brought you here as a way of cleansing Sumtoa of evil."

"Tell the King that I am grateful to be of service," I said, "and that any of his people that wish to sail with us are free to do so, and that we will return with supplies and other men to help protect all of you."

Rarahu repeated this to the King, and the King replied.

"King Vaea says that we will be here as spirits on the wind, joining the gods in a great journey. He says that you will hear his voice on the wind, and his voice and the voice of all of his people will push the sails of your ship to safety, and that you will hear us whenever you wish to listen."

Before I could reply, we were interrupted by one of Rarahu's riflemen who spoke urgently in a hushed tone.

"The Uhaite are attacking," Rarahu announced, "and they have slain some cattle. In a short while the lava flow will prevent them from coming closer. Take your treasure and go! My men will handle the Uhaite."

But I wasn't ready to visit the treasure cave. I organized my men in preparation for the trek to the beach. I split everyone into groups. I had Dusty, Tehani, Edgar, Lani and her father in the first group, and Johnny, Satina, Edgar, Rocco and myself following a short distance behind. I didn't want us clumped together. Rocco and I would move back and forth between the groups in reconnaissance formation. Badoo, as always, was our dependable albeit unseen ally.

I was told once by a professional gambler in a Tasmanian pub that both good luck and bad luck happen in threes. He told me that you can only wait and ride it out, because nothing could change the outcome. The Uhaite attacking was the second part of our bad luck; and I was experiencing the first of three stages of anger toward Victoria. My mood was foul.

The Uhaite were far more resourceful than we had anticipated. A sudden volley of frantic gunfire convinced Rocco and me to join Rarahu. We cut through the jungle and hiked to the valley's edge. The Uhaite had disemboweled several Zebu and had stopped to gorge themselves. We were greeted by the ghastly site of the beast-men gnawing at the Zebu flesh, covered in blood, their faces contorted in the ecstasy of gluttony, a crimson sneer carved on their gore-splattered lips.

The hot flame of my anger grew stronger. I wanted to kill them all; I wanted to see these monsters vanquished once and for all. I pulled my gun and shot one of them just as he raised his head and saw me. Rocco grabbed my arm.

"Leave it, captain. Rarahu and his men will take care of these bastards."

Rarahu himself was waving us on, shouting for us to go. I reluctantly stepped back. Rocco was almost pushing me, trying to get me to turn around. I heard him shouting "Let's get the damn treasure and get to the ship." Just then a group of the Uhaite suddenly burst from the jungle behind us. We didn't have time to react. We were stuck between the two Uhaite groups. They unleashed their spears, taking us by surprise. Rarahu, jumping forward, pushed me aside and took a spear in his belly. I saw the bloody tip of the spear jutting from his left lower back as he went down on one knee. He had saved my life, either inadvertently or by design.

Rarahu shouted to his men as he went down, never once showing any sign of pain or despair. One of his men handed him a flintlock rifle which he raised and fired in one smooth motion, killing the beast-man that had speared him. He toppled sideways and never moved again.

Rocco let loose with a string of profanity in both English and Italian. I emptied the .45 into the bellowing crowd of savage beast-men. Rocco emptied his .45 as well, and then we were moving past them. In my memory, it all seems to happen in slow-motion; but in reality it was but a few minutes.

I slammed a fresh clip into my .45, kicking a wounded beast-man in the face as I strode past him. Rarahu's men had reacted quickly, firing and re-loading in practiced syncopation. We dashed into the jungle, my stomach in knots and overcome with anger.

Victoria had caused Rarahu's death, dear Victoria, and I was going to make her suffer. All I could think about was avenging Rarahu when another eruption shook the ground beneath our feet.

The heat from the outpouring of lava was intense. I glanced up at the mountainside and saw blistering hot red streams of lava curling out of the rock as if possessed by an evil spirit.

I stumbled and almost fell, catching myself at the last moment. Looking over my shoulder, I saw the Sumtoan riflemen continuing their barrage against the Uhaite. The rumbling beneath the earth was growing louder. The trail curved to our left, toward the village, and I still thought it was possible that we might get back to our ship.

However, I had a score to settle. So did Rocco.

We were of one mind now; get off the island, but not before finding Victoria.

"I'm going to kill that bitch," Rocco vowed under his breath.

My heart was pounding nearly out of my chest as I reached the village's perimeter at the same moment when the rumbling increased in volume.

The air was now filling slowly with ash. It danced on the breeze like dirty snow. I saw the plume of smoke high atop the volcano wavering insanely in the tropic thermals.

There were three phases of the attack, and there were three phases to my anger. I understand this now only as I wrote these words. It is as clear in my mind as if a diagram had been drawn. My anger had flared to life but had yet to reach its hottest point; and while their attack had been clumsily initiated, the outcome on their behalf still seemed inevitable.

At the center of this stood Victoria, an image in my mind now of a greedy tart. In those hallucinatory and anguished moments after Rarahu's death, I saw her as something far less than the exotic image she presented to newspapermen; she was no better than a spoiled child demanding more and still more. The words that I am writing cannot adequately express my anger. Let me state without equivocation that it was my anger that drove me onward.

We were in the village center, standing in the street when the Chinese riflemen came down from the rocks and attacked in a mad rush. Simultaneously, the Uhaite came at us in swarms, all of them. Rarahu's men were disorganized, his iron-like presence now missing, and they were perhaps too grief stricken to react properly. Yet they tried to rally, and I admired them for it.

I shot a beast-man in the left eye and it popped like exploding fruit. His jaw dropped open, and he fell back screaming before he died. The street was chaotic. Turoa had appeared from nowhere wielding a sword. He fought viciously, swinging the sword with a precision that comes with practice. A beast-man's head was severed and rolled into the street pinwheeling blood. Another head sailed past me; the eyes and mouth open in stupefied amazement before hitting the wall next to me with a sickening thud.

They were coming at us from all directions, and Rocco and I were the focal point of an angry melee. I don't know how we survived the next few minutes. I cannot attribute our survival to skill.

My instincts told me to retreat, but I still had to get my crew on their way. Johnny and Dusty were hunkered down in opposite doorways, taking aim at either a Chinese pirate or a beast-man as the opportunity presented itself. I had glimpses of Rocco and Turoa battling one foe after another.

Two Uhaite charged me. I shot them both, but they didn't go down. I emptied the remainder of the clip into one of them. Before I could snap in a fresh clip, I was struck down. This time I hung onto my gun. He might have had me if something resembling intelligence had lurked between his ears, but his stupidity and my anger spelled his doom. He began kicking and pummeling me from a crouched position, which naturally lessened the impact of his blows.

I ejected the clip and slammed in a fresh clip, yanked the slide back and twisted about on my back and fired. The bullet hit his head, jerking him upward, and then he fell over onto his side. I heard his death rattle as I lurched to my feet.

Rocco was yelling at me.

"Inside! Come on!"

He pulled me toward a doorway and shoved me inside. This was one of the buildings where the Sumtoans had made wooden doors, and they braced it shut with a cross-beam as we ducked inside. King Vaea and his wife Oleka were chanting and singing. With Rarahu dead, that left only Turoa and professor Kawena to translate. We had lost sight of Turoa during the sudden street fight. In the end, it wouldn't matter. King Vaea wasn't leaving. He had placed his faith in whatever god he believed in, and I wish now that his dreams are realized, and that King Vaea and his people are in a better place.

Since the buildings were connected, we darted into an adjoining hovel. It wouldn't fool the Chinese for long, but at the moment there were more confused Uhaite clamoring to find a way in than there were Chinese. We took advantage of their confusion to slip up the street and emerge near the highest elevation point before the village was displaced by volcanic rock.

This was nearly our undoing. No sooner had we emerged from the building than the Chinese opened fire on us. They had anticipated our deceptive retreat and had turned around to wait for us to exit the building. Their bullets tore holes into the wall next to my head, missing me by a fraction of an inch. I felt the swish of hot air as the bullets whizzed past my head.

Rocco and I dodged and stumbled backward into the shadowy doorway. Desperate to find a way out, we climbed out a rear window, which bordered the last vestiges of jungle that abutted the volcanic wall.

We stopped short, stunned by the sight of a massive lava flowing burning an inexorable path downhill and into the jungle. Some of the hellish lava was already dangerously close to the back end of the village. Very soon, the village itself would be devoured by the endless and immensely powerful lava flow.

I felt a hollow, sinking feeling as a wave of despair washed over me.

"Captain, look!"

Rocco was pointing up into the rocks where the Chinese riflemen had begun their attack. Zhang Chen was standing up in those rocks, his features showing no emotion, his stare hard, his eyes unblinking. He was looking at me the way a scientist examines a heretofore unknown species of mollusk, and I didn't like that at all. He didn't look fearful, and he didn't look as if he intended to attack us. He simply watched us, and my uneasiness grew with each passing second. What was with this bastard?

I knew he was too far away, and I sensed that he had planned that, too. I was a good shot with a .45 automatic, a very good shot. But a shot uphill at approximately a hundred yards with a handgun was pushing my luck. I didn't care. I wanted him dead. I had the gun in my hand and I braced my left palm underneath the grip to hold my arm steady, sighted down the barrel, and fired once. I had calculated the windage and the declining arc of the lead, so I shot high. The gun bucked in my hand.

My shot splintered the rocks half a foot to his left, at which point he mildly turned his head and studied the dust that had risen where my bullet had struck. He looked back at me, and I swear, even at that distance, I thought I detected a faint smile.

He disappeared when I blinked. He was like a phantom that was there one moment and gone the next. The profanity that flung from my lips was equal to any curse that Rocco had ever uttered.

Alarmed by the increasing lava, we re-grouped and I set in motion our final actions. With the street overrun by pirates and beast-men, I ordered Dusty and Johnny to retreat through the jungle, and cut down through the valley where the Zebu had grazed. It was a long way around, but there was no other choice.

We had to fight our way out of the village. The Uhaite had broken in and were searching the buildings while the pirates contented themselves to preventing our escape by guarding the main street. I saw Rocco yank a spear from a beast-man's hands and ram it through his chest. I shot several beasts as I held the rear formation, allowing my crew to exit the village.

During the confusion, we experienced several tremors and rumblings as the volcano continued making its presence known. We made it out of the village; all thoughts of taking any treasure now vanished. Our goal was survival.

This was no orderly exit, but we still might have made it. Doc and Edgar had managed to take the lead, followed by Dusty and Tehani. The professor and Lani were together and separated from Johnny and Satina by fifty yards. Progress was slow. Rocco and I were far back, winging shots at any beast-men that appeared behind us.

We heard the deep rumbling and felt the ground shake before the explosion. The air was suddenly suffused with noxious particles, and I felt as if the wind had been knocked from my lungs. I was knocked off my feet. The eruption opened the earth in front of us, and in one instant I saw Satina turn and grab Johnny as the earth yawned open like the mouth of a hungry demon. A gigantic burst of lava consumed them in a split second, covering them completely, and the lava took command of the earth like a serpent born in fire.

FOURTEEN

Lani and Tehani were screaming. For a moment I thought they had been killed, but when I was able to see across the lava pit they were being pulled away by Doc and Edgar. The professor's leg was badly burned, but he was able to walk. I shouted at Dusty to move as fast as possible and get to the ship. Dusty knew what to do, and so did Doc and Edgar.

Rocco and I were cut off and would have to get out the hard way. I swallowed my grief and willed myself to be strong. Another hallucinatory moment ensued when we again entered the building and passed King Vaea and his wife Oleka sitting at the table holding hands and chanting. We never saw them again.

I heard the distant burst of a Thompson machinegun; our first indication in some time that Badoo was alive and still raising hell. At that point, I was too grief-stricken and too angry to give Badoo much thought.

We walked out onto the street with anger burning inside me unlike any anger I have ever experienced. I shot a pirate in the belly, holstered my gun, pulled the Arisaka rifle from his hands and caved his skull in with it. Another pirate, seeing what I had done, attempted to swing his own rifle around but Rocco shot him in the knee. Tossing aside the bloody rifle I had clubbed his shipmate with, I jerked his rifle from his hands and used it to calmly shoot several other pirates who were trying to hide by dashing into the jungle. My shots cut them down, and then I dropped the empty rifle in front of the pirate holding his shattered knee. There wasn't enough time for medical attention, and we were content to let him bleed out. He stared at us in horror, his bloody fingers unable to stanch the blood that gushed from the destroyed bone that shone with a crimson sheen. Rocco and I would not deliver a merciful death, not in our frame of mind.

I saw Thad Bellamy far up the hill, heading toward the treasure cave. We knew that Victoria had to be nearby, and we knew where they were going.

"Let's follow that weasel," Rocco said.

But following Thad Bellamy was easier said than done. Another metallic detonation from the Thompson indicated that Badoo was coming in our direction. He appeared to be in the jungle, across the lava stream. With the full force of Zhang Chen's pirates attacking us, we reluctantly retreated yet again into a building.

I was blind with rage. Playing a cat and mouse game from inside a building infuriated me all the more. I wanted to destroy them all, and I wanted the immediate satisfaction of seeing them die. We had been forced into a combat position that offered little opportunity for a tactical advantage.

The air was filled with the constant sound of gunfire mingled now with the satanic roar of the earth welcoming us to hell as the volcano shook us mercilessly. The lava stream had widened in sections and was encroaching on the town itself. We had a hard time breathing because the air was growing dense with smoke.

I realize only now what am amazing sight we witnessed when we emerged again onto the jungle's periphery behind the village. Badoo had killed a pirate, lifted his body above his head and tossed it onto the lava stream. In the next instant he dashed forward, leaping onto the flaming body as if it were a stepping-stone and hurtling himself across the widening lava flow.

There was no time to marvel at his Olympian feat. Rocco asked him how much ammo he had and Badoo said the canister was half-empty. That was enough for us. He swung the Thompson off his shoulder strap and we went back out to the street. Zhang Chen's pirates had taken the village. They were everywhere.

The ensuing street fight defines a madness that is held in the hearts of all men; an evil that simmers in our souls and turns us into loathsome creatures. We killed the Chinese pirates, and we killed the straggling Uhaite beast-men. Badoo and the Thompson made short work of the bastards. As I have already described, a Thompson sub-machinegun is one of the more lethal weapons created by mankind, and the bullets

...we were content to let him bleed out.

turned them into bloody piles of twitching meat. In my madness and in my anger, I felt no sympathy and no remorse. I am not proud of the killing, but when I think about Johnny and Satina, and of the peace-loving people that lived on Sumtoa Island, I am content at being a murderer. When it was over, the blood ran in rivulets down the street and the moans of the dying fell on deaf ears.

We brought Badoo up to date and I sent him after the crew. He took the remaining Thompson cartridges from the rucksack, and I gave him a revolver taken from one of the dead pirates. There was no time for anything else. Badoo slipped away, and I trusted his ability to catch up with the others. Rocco refused to follow Badoo and said he would see this through with me to the end, so we went after Bellamy and Victoria.

There were still some pirates running about; and at the same time the canopy of volcanic cloud that hung over the island was like a dark shroud threatening to smother us all. There are moments here where everything is a blur, or I don't remember events at all. I recall killing a Chinese man with my bare hands. I think he stumbled into us, and I spun around and caved his nose in with my fist. I think I enjoyed killing him, and Rocco may have kicked him furiously once he was on the ground. Rocco said I was screaming at any pirates we encountered, even the dead ones, and I turned a wounded pirate's head to pulp with the butt of his own rifle.

I do recall at one point believing that I was already dead; that I had been killed and now roamed the earth as an avenging angel. I was invincible because I was dead, and I told the remaining pirates I was a dead man returned to life and they would suffer terribly because of this. I was true to my word about them suffering.

I thought I was dead and because I was dead, I had lost Lani. I realize now I had gone mad, of course, and Rocco told me later I was a fearsome sight. When we reached the red door leading to the treasure cave we killed three pirates quickly, and with such ferocity they were screaming in terror as they died. I am not certain, but I may have disemboweled a man with his own knife, cut off a length of his intestine and shoved it into another man's mouth before I shot him. Rocco has asked me never to bring these moments up or talk about them again, and he believes we may have put a curse on ourselves.

We entered the building and immediately noticed the jade Buddha was missing. Victoria had been here. We climbed the ladder and found a flickering torch still set in a sconce on the wall. Rocco took the torch, and we climbed the ladder. The flickering light revealed an over-turned table and treasure strewn about. There was still plenty of treasure left, although Victoria and Bellamy had taken a great deal. I barely noticed the glimmering sapphires and Roman coins lying in heaps on the floor as we traveled up the length of that dark tunnel toward the cliffside trail.

A series of fluctuating tremors motivated us out of that tunnel before it became our graves; and when we smelled the salt-spray of the sea, we thankfully emerged onto the winding precipice overlooking the boiling surf.

We saw Victoria immediately. She was quite some distance along the cliffside ledge and struggling with four large burlap sacks. In her greed, she had filled those sacks with too much treasure. Further along we saw Bellamy, and Rocco said he would stop him. Victoria saw us and came to a standstill. She had a sack in each hand, one slung over each shoulder. I was casually impressed at her endurance.

Rocco said, "Just shoot her." He slipped past her and went after Bellamy so swiftly that Victoria barely had time to blink. I heard her curse. She was good at cursing. She dropped the bags.

In my memory, I can see her bathed in a solitary fragment of silver light that broke free of the volcanic clouds and framed her in its glow. There she was, this attractive creature as I had first met her, smiling at me as a dazzling portrait of classical beauty, enticing and impossible for any man to ignore, and she was born unto this world like Eve to entice Adam, and the flow of time is forever changed by her embrace. Then a thousand shades of fluttering gray and purple mingled with the volcanic ash to extinguish the light, and her bright eyes were shaded by dark shapes.

I stood transfixed, trying to both decipher and hold the impress of this occurrence in my memory, and I am haunted now to remember such details as they once were, evil shadows on a bright landscape, all joined forever with the crashing sound of the sea and the persistent roar of an angry volcano.

"Elliot, you're covered in blood."

"Damn you."

"Go back and take some treasure. There's plenty left. You can have all of it. There's more than Thad and I can carry. Go on, Elliot."

"Do you know what you've done?"

"Of course, you fool, I've made myself very wealthy."

"You were wealthy before you came here. Do you need all of this wealth? What will you do with it?"

She gave a little laugh, but it was hollow and forced.

"Do you feel the ground shaking? Go home, Elliot. Go home to New York and your museum and your fossils. You're like them, a fossil, a relic from some bygone era, and you'll never fit in. Never."

Her words stung me. I had no response. I recall trying to think of something to say, but I was assailed by a sudden and overwhelming fatigue.

The volcano intervened and a massive eruption turned the world topsy-turvy. The eruption knocked me to the ground. I lost sight of Victoria as the world spun beneath me. I heard her shriek.

"God-damn you, Elliot!"

She was knocked to the edge by the eruption, and for a second I thought it was over. I thought Victoria had been flung over the cliffside, but somehow she had found a hand-hold. I crawled over the dropped treasure bags and saw her manicured fingers clutching at an outcropping. I pulled myself to my feet and looked down at her. She was hanging on, but there was scant area for her to place her feet onto a ledge. The surf crashed wildly on the rocks far below her.

"Help me up, damn you!"

This woman had caused all of this madness. Her actions had resulted in the deaths of Johnny and Satina and of Rarahu, and so many more. I wanted to kill her. I thought about killing her with pleasure. She dangled for an eternity, her face red from her effort, her fingers barely able to grip the slippery rock.

"Elliot, pull me up!"

Her voice was pleading, but I stood there and only looked at her, numb with grief and exhausted beyond words. I could hear the maddening surf crashing on the rocks below, and when the volcano offered another rumble. I saw Victoria's eyes go wide with fear.

"Elliot, what are you waiting for?! Pull me up!"

"It's because of you that Johnny is dead," I said.

"What are you talking about? Pull me up!"

She was trying desperately to dig her fingernails into the volcanic rock and gain leverage, but it was no use. I would have to pull her up. Then her face changed and her anger came alive once more.

"You dirty bastard!" she hissed. "I'm glad they're dead! The treasure is mine! It was always meant to be mine!"

Then she let go with her right hand and pulled the revolver from her holster. This took an extraordinary effort on her part, her face pinched from her strenuous exertions, and as she dangled by one hand, she meant to shoot me. I saw her trying to swing the gun up and aim it.

My boot stomped her left hand. My reaction was pure reflex, a survival instinct, or maybe that's what I'm telling myself now. I heard the bones in her hand crack as my boot dug into her hand. She screamed.

For an incredible second she was suspended in the air, and then she dropped swiftly, her eyes glazed with fear as she comprehended what had occurred. She screamed all the way down, and I saw her body strike the rocks, her brains dashed across the stones, and she was instantly lifeless. I stared numbly as the sea rose up, the waves curling like the fingers of an ancient witch, and they plucked Victoria's body from the rocks and pulled her down into the unforgiving depths of Neptune's kingdom.

FIFTEEN

"She's dead, captain. It's time to go."

Rocco had come up beside me, and he pulled me away from the edge. I was staring at the sea and listening to the sea's endless cacophony, like cymbals crashing relentlessly against the unyielding shore, the wicked waves mocking me.

Rocco picked up Victoria's treasure bags, and insisted we carry the treasure to the ship. I doubted very much that we would live to enjoy any of it. Together we made the grim trek along the ledge. All the while I felt that Victoria was watching me from beneath those tumultuous green waves, her gaze piercing me with the sharpness of a knife. Down we went along that precarious ledge as the earth buckled and rumbled.

Everything is a blur to me. We had hoped that our comrades were alive. Lani had to be alive. I could not accept that they had failed, and so Rocco and I were eager to rejoin our shipmates.

"Where's Bellamy?"

"He got away, but he won't get far."

We proceeded as voyagers into the unknown and fully expecting an attack. The fact that we continued to survive is now a source of amazement to me. Somehow, we made it clear of that ledge before it collapsed, and we ventured all too slowly into the jungle below the village.

The circuitous jungle path was oddly calm. The greenery was bustling with sounds; the bird calls and scrambling of frightened animals created a constant din. The sweat was pouring off us. Still my tired legs kept moving, but I was near the breaking point of exhaustion.

I thought our trek through the jungle would never end. The heat and smoke had stifled us, and our breathing was labored. Rocco never complained, but trudged ever onward, while I may have given in to the temptation to soundly curse the world. We walked and walked, the two wealthiest murderers in history, and this thought struck me as humorous. I began laughing. Rocco told me to shut-up, but my maniacal laugh continued to ring out.

Rocco held my arm and told me to drop the sacks of treasure. We stood there beneath the wavering green canopy while Rocco produced a flask of whiskey. That he would still have a small measure of whiskey remaining also struck me as humorous, but I took a long swallow. This produced a long welcome effect of warmth spreading through my belly. Rocco told me to finish the flask, and so I did. There were three good swallows remaining, and the whiskey jolted me with a hot punch.

I can't say I had a spring in my step after that, but it was enough to have me stumble along while helping Rocco carry several million dollars in treasure. We arrived at a shady area to rest a few moments in the cool green shadows. Then we again encountered the lowlands where the Komodo dragons lived.

Thad Bellamy decided to ambush us here, at the periphery of the grasslands.

We heard the sound of his gun as a bullet whizzed over our heads, smacked a glancing blow on a tree before tumbling into the undergrowth. We didn't have time to flinch. We stopped and looked at each other. Rocco's skin was dripping sweat from every pore. His shirt was soaked, as if he had been swimming. He looked more irritated than angry.

"He could have killed one of us if he'd taken his time," he cursed.

"I don't see him."

"Let's put these sacks down and kill him."

We stowed the treasure behind some limp ferns and crouched in a jigsaw of purple flowers and stared out at the marsh. Another bullet went crashing into the jungle, but further to our right. We scanned the area until we spotted him. He was on our left, not all that far away, which made his marksmanship all the more laughable.

"It's a .38." Rocco noted. "He's desperate."

Rocco and I pulled our guns. We took our sweet time aiming. Rocco and I have logged hundreds, perhaps thousands, of hours practicing with a Colt .45 automatic. The U.S. Army considers us expert marksmen. Rocco and I have both trained top military brass in handgun target shooting, albeit off the books and in secret. I had only the slightest view of Thad Bellamy who remained partially screened by a stumpy tree.

I emptied the Colt's clip. Rocco emptied his Colt.

The brass pinged into the grass and the receivers on our guns recoiled, leaving the hot muzzles exhaling blue smoke. We ejected our clips and slammed in fresh clips.

Bellamy had disappeared. There was no sound but for the cawing and shrill shouts of birds high in the jungle canopy.

"We should check the body," I said.

"Or take his treasure, but we can't carry more than this."

"Leave it."

So we left Bellamy to rot and began the slow trek around the swamp. We followed the identical path we had arrived on; circling the area where we knew the Komodo dragons thrived.

We trudged under a mountain of ash that filled the sky with darkness. The ash cloud was like some living thing that towered above us and passed judgment on us. We had angered the dark gods. We moved by instinct alone. Our bodies had failed us and our limbs struggled with their exertions. I was without hope, but I forced myself to move. Rocco moved grimly and silently next to me.

We had reached the halfway point without encountering any Komodo dragons when a familiar voice shouted behind me.

"Captain, be careful!"

There was no urgency in the words; it was a simple declaration. I turned around but there was no one there. Confused, I looked at Rocco.

"What are you looking at?" He asked.

Then we heard a Komodo dragon thrashing about in the wetlands. A shriek filled the air, followed by a gunshot. We waited. Thad Bellamy had survived although he was mortally wounded. The fool had come across the marsh instead of circling about. We saw him knee deep in a stagnant pool and surround by two Komodo dragons. The dragons were irritated by the constant trembling from the volcano, and naturally they were hungry. Bellamy was covered in blood. Our bullets had found their mark. That he had come this far with such grievous wounds was remarkable.

He was cussing and shooting at the Komodo dragons. When he fired his last shot and the hammer clacked harmlessly on the cylinder, he bellowed in anguish and threw his gun at the closest dragon.

A Komodo dragon came up behind him. It caught his leg in its jaw and pulled him down. The other dragon scampered onto Bellamy with ease. We watched as the dragons tore Bellamy to bits, fascinated by the carnage. Bellamy's head was torn off his body, discarded, and his limbs ripped loose in a frenzy. I felt not one ounce of sympathy.

In fact, the horrible scene revitalized me. Bellamy and Victoria had both reached a well-deserved end. Maybe the dark gods weren't so bad after all.

We made haste and entered the last stretch of jungle. We passed the missionary's hut without a second glance, intent on breaking free of the stifling heat. We sensed the beach before we saw it; a lingering tendril of fresh air teased us.

The scene that greeted us upon pushing free of the jungle will be forever etched in my mind. My crew had survived, and they had waited for us on the beach. Badoo simply stepped forward with Lani and they took the sacks from us and placed them in the longboat. Lani had tears in her eyes. I pulled her close to me for a moment, reveling in the warmth of her body and the tenderness of her soul. Doc and Edgar muttered something about us taking our sweet time. Dusty and Tehani had climbed into the boat along with Professor Kawena.

It was Badoo that pointed out the last problem facing us.

The Chinese sloop had anchored in the bay near us. The Kraken had risen again and latched itself to the sloop. The Chinese were desperately attempting to extricate the Kraken from their ship. Its tendrils had suctioned onto the side and one of them was tangled in a mast. The sloop rocked back and forth, both from the Kraken and from the series of tremors that shook the bay with each volcanic twinge.

The Chinese were aware of our presence but were too deeply involved in battling the Kraken to bother with us. I was aware of the cannon mounted on their deck. That would prove our undoing if they thought to use it on us.

We pushed off in the longboat, Badoo at the oars. A fierce thirst had taken hold of me. I think of this now with perplexity. The mind recalls the oddest details during moments of stress. I was thirsty, and I was praying for the Kraken to sink the Chinese sloop.

The volcanic eruptions had resumed, although they were not a strong as the previous ones. We were still challenged, however, by the choppy water. I kept my eye on the Chinese pirates. With each eruption a wave came over the bow and slapped us with a warm sea-shower. Soaked and exhausted, Badoo pressed on, his muscles bulging with effort. I so admired him at that moment. He offered not the slightest indication of concern, focused instead on rowing us toward our ship.

The longboat was roughly tossed about as Lani hung onto me. We appeared to be moving far too slowly. I despaired that we weren't making any progress, but eventually we moved closer to *The Reaper's Scythe.*

As we drew closer to our ship, I saw Zhang Chen standing on the sloop's deck and watching us. It was an eerie sight; he was surrounded by pandemonium as his men attacked the Kraken with spears and guns, all of which had minimal effect on the giant creature. Zhang Chen had his eyes locked on me, unblinking, his features a riddle that I could not decipher. We rowed past him and came up to our ship. In a painstakingly slow process, we disembarked from the longboat and climbed aboard the ship.

We took the women below, and Rocco and I went to engine room while Badoo and Dusty remained on deck after arming themselves with fresh rifles. Even with his busted arm, Dusty had managed to prove he was still an accurate sharpshooter. It was only after we had started the diesel engine that I realized the error Zhang Chen had made by not leaving a contingent aboard our ship. He had to know it too, not that it would have made a difference.

In fifteen agonizing minutes, we had the engine started. We were about an hour from high tide, but my on-the-spot plan was to ride the crest of a wave as the eruptions shook the lagoon. It wasn't a brilliant idea.

As the eruptions increased, we made a short circle and pointed the bow at the lagoon's entrance. All this time the madness continued aboard the Chinese sloop and Zhang Chen watched us with those penetrating eyes. The high tide had begun but we weren't confident we could ride the crest of a wave without scraping the coral reef. In fact, we did scrape the reef, but the damage to the ship was minimal. *The Reaper's Scythe* slid past the Chinese sloop, exited the lagoon with a heavy bump, and wandered out into the turbulent sea.

Sumtoa Island was in turmoil. The steady belching of ash and lava from the volcano had already changed the island's topography, and the eruptions were increasing at an alarming rate. We had escaped, but all of us were too exhausted and too numb to do anything but stare at the island as it receded into the distance.

Lani came onto deck with Dusty and Tehani and we stood at the rail. Both Lani and Tehani were weeping softly. For a moment, I was overwhelmed by the thought that I had lost something; that something had been torn from me, and that my very soul had been wounded. Whatever I had lost, I could never regain.

We retreated to Bora Bora, and shortly afterward Sumtoa Island exploded with a force the equal of Krakatoa's destruction. We might have been lost in the resulting tsunami had Bora Bora not served as a shield. We only recently learned that the sound of Sumtoa Island exploding could be heard over three thousand miles away. The steam and ash that had been released into the atmosphere turned the sky dark for days. We don't know yet how much of the island is still visible, if any, but we are eager for any reports from traveling freighters who pass that area.

After initiating repairs and purchasing provisions, we traveled to Tasmania and disembarked at Sandy Bay. There are some pubs with good food and a quiet and respectable population, and we did nothing more than rest for several weeks. Tasmania was a salve for our injured souls.

We also took inventory of the treasure, which is substantial. The wealth was divided equally with the exception of a larger portion set aside for Johnny Turner's family. Johnny left a brother who is a year younger, and an ailing father.

Badoo had chosen to remain aboard the *The Reaper's Scythe* where he spent his evenings on deck looking at the sky. I visited him once a day and he spoke of portents and omens, and a future that he said might test us all. He was unusually grim. I left him to his mystic musings, and I silently prayed that he was wrong. I thought we had all been tested enough already.

I had not spoken to any of them about the voice I heard in the marsh before Thad Bellamy was killed. I may never speak of it at all again. It was Johnny's voice that I heard, as clear as a ship's bell.

We travelled to Singapore again, and I used my contacts at the British consulate's office to dispatch a general report. Eventually we intend on returning to Hawaii, which I will make my new base of operations. Dusty and Tehani have decided to settle in Oklahoma, with their fortune to assist them, and I pray their future is bright.

A few days ago I dreamed that I met Johnny and Satina on some distant island, but they were older. Johnny had gray at his temples, and Satina was heavier. They were quite happy and greeted me amiably. Badoo once told me that there is a spirit world next to ours, and that to reach it takes but a few steps, but he couldn't tell me if those steps were the right steps or the wrong steps. So I meet my fallen friends again often in my dreams, and when I look out across the sea I wonder how close they are, or how far away?

We never escaped the sea. It is at our feet every day, a mocking presence threatening to drag us into its undertow. The dead move through my restless sleep like schools of yellow fish making abstract patterns in the wavering eelgrass on the sea's floor. The fronds of this ocean grass are beckoning to me across the expanse of time, and I cannot escape its allure. I am caught in a tropical current that is all too familiar; dangerous but deceptively comfortable in its warmth. I am hanging in the current, and Victoria swims toward me with her ghastly smile. At other times, I dream that I see Johnny on the foredeck, and I ask him if he has been avenged, but he never answers me. He is a will-o-the-wisp slipping past me without acknowledgment, and my question is answered by his silence.

The waves of the sea are endless, and the moon tides hold us in sway. The waves curl toward us so gently; and then recede gently, ebbing and flowing timelessly; ebbing and flowing...

EPILOGUE

Bill Harrison closed the leather-bound journal and took a long pull of bourbon straight from the bottle. He stood up, pulling a Chesterfield from the packet. He smoked the cigarette staring out at the sea. The day had waned and the undulating sea was mesmerizing. A soft, deceptive breeze slipped in over the railing, and the light on the water was glazed with a ceramic quality that was as deceptive as the breeze. Harrison knew he would never think of the sea in the same way again.

"Badoo was right," Elliot Graves said behind him. "We were tested again and again. The war tested all of us."

"You were right, of course, I can't publish this."

"You'll think of something," Graves said, "something that will satisfy your editor."

"They wouldn't believe it about the Kraken, or about those Chinese pirates. It's a good thing they were killed."

"No, they weren't killed."

Harrison turned and looked at Graves with surprise.

"But the Kraken had taken hold of their ship?"

"Somehow they escaped, and Zhang Chen chased us across the seven seas. I almost killed him in '44. That's when he lost a leg. I finally ended the bastard's life fourteen months ago."

Graves picked up the leather-bound journal and placed it with the other journals on his bookcase. Harrison's eyes swept across the room. The clay tablets, the journals, the Mauser rifle—everything here had a purpose and a history. Harrison noticed a small photograph in a varnished wood frame. He recognized Graves, Rocco and Lani. The tall dark man was obviously Badoo.

Graves noticed him scrutinizing the photograph. "That's the only photograph we have of Johnny and Satina." Graves pointed to the couple on the right.

"And what became of the rest of your crew?"

"We lost Doc in '44 when we encountered a Jap sub. He was killed by machine-gun fire." Graves gestured to the Japanese sword on the shelf. "I took that off the submarine's captain after I killed him."

An uncomfortable silence descended on the room. Harrison wasn't certain what to say next, and he was relieved when Lani entered the room.

"I've prepared dinner," she said pleasantly, and she smiled. Harrison was looking at her with a new perspective as well. He had to work hard to avoid staring at the red diamonds set in a silver pendant that hung on a chain and glimmered in her ample cleavage. He followed them into the dining room.

Rocco sat with them, and shortly they were joined by two children. Harrison wasn't surprised when Lani introduced them as John and Satina. The boy and girl were about a year apart, maybe nine and ten, rambunctious but still possessing manners. They were served fresh lobster, rice pilaf, vegetables, and diced yellow potatoes with butter, fresh wheat bread, and for desert a bowl each of scooped vanilla ice-cream laced with caramel and pineapple slices.

The dinner conversation was steered toward the children, and there was some small talk about the tourist business. Harrison picked up on the idea to avoid any discussion about the past. He was conscious of Rocco studying him from time to time. After dinner, Lani wished Harrison well and took the children out. Harrison joined Graves with Rocco in the den where they sat on the porch and smoked cigars.

"Badoo returned to Africa," Graves told him, "I understand he has a reputation now. He's a game warden intent on stopping the slaughter of elephants for ivory. He opened a wildlife sanctuary and promotes safaris for photographers, so he started a trend."

"I wouldn't cross him, that's for sure," Rocco chuckled.

"Edgar owns a five-star restaurant here in Honolulu, and Dusty took Tehani home to Oklahoma. He has a horse ranch and three kids. That keeps him busy."

Harrison nodded. "I'm at a loss for words."

"I have a friend named Don Blanding," Graves said, "you may have heard of him. He finds creative ways to mend his soul, just as we all must."

The statement surprised Harrison who hadn't expected to learn so many personal details about Captain Graves.

"You said you were on Guadalcanal," Rocco remembered.

"That's right. It was tough. I don't know what else to say about it."

"You don't have to say anything." Rocco smiled slightly and poured half a glass of bourbon for Harrison and handed it to him. They drank their bourbon and smoked their cigars as the twilight shimmered across the whitecaps tugging at the beach below them. Harrison felt that he had crossed some type of threshold.

"That man you knew on Guadalcanal, Richard Knox, he was undoubtedly part of Victoria's crew."

"I don't know how to tell your story," Harrison admitted.

Graves pointed to his bookshelves. "You see that. I read all the time. Some of this science fiction stuff is amazing. I read a book by Robert A. Heinlein called *Space Cadet*. I gave it my son, and he loved it. Now he wants to become a pilot and maybe one day to travel in space."

"Just make something up," Rocco said, "and whoever you base on me had better be the hero."

They laughed, Harrison suddenly realized what these men were doing for him, and he was grateful. An hour later, they all shook hands. Graves and Rocco wished Harrison well, and asked that he keep in touch. Harrison went out into the night knowing that reading the journal of Elliot Graves had changed him. His ambition had grown in him, nurtured by his knowing these men and their story.

Harrison was in a kind of trance as he walked. Against a background of neon and the clamoring bleat of automobile horns, he blended into the downtown crowd, overwhelmed by the scent of sweat and diesel fumes, and the incessant laughter of joyous couples on a night out. Passing an alley, he became aware of the slanting dangerous shadows that spelled danger; and he picked up the enticing scent of a woman's perfume. He paused near a diner where two women stood talking near the revolving door. They wore clean-pressed dresses and carried little black purses that dangled from their arms on chains as they smoked their cigarettes. He could hear them talking about perfume, Max Factor's Hypnotique, which they said was better priced than Chanel No. 5. "I want to be kissed when I wear perfume," one woman said, "that's what it's all about, honey. Put on just enough so that he wants to kiss you."

He stopped at the hotel bar and drank whiskey chased by cold beer. He cut back on his smoking and just drank for a while. His mind was filled with the Kraken's tentacles, beast-men in the jungle, red diamonds and the soft flesh of a beautiful woman.

Bill Harrison did not sleep that night. *I have survived Guadalcanal*, he thought, *and that has to mean something.*

That morning he started typing on his portable Remington. He wrote a feature about Captain Elliot Graves that only mentioned Victoria Ransom in one paragraph, and he deflected everything, but it was detailed enough so that his editor should bite on it. Not one word was true, but it wasn't exactly a lie. Harrison knew what he was going to do next. It took him some time. He worked at it. He wrote three pages and read them, and crinkled them up and tossed them in the waste-basket. He started over. He wrote for some time, hammering the typewriter keys. He changed all the names and kept writing. He knew then that he was about to become a paperback fiction writer, and it felt good.

He had it then. The words flowed from his fingertips and found life through the typewriter keys. His typing made a steady staccato sound that caught the warm breeze and drifted from his hotel window. He saw the story in his mind's eye, and he could put Guadalcanal there, too, right in the first chapter; and Honolulu was bristling with life right in front of him, so he added Honolulu. There was a glimpse of the Luau girls in those tight flower-print sarongs and the taste of bourbon and the smell of tobacco. Then he found his way to Singapore in 1936, and he began following a crooked alleyway that led to a seafront saloon. He had the story then and his fingers slapped the keys persistently. Punching the carriage return, he began another line, grinning to himself.

He was going to need more paper.

THE END

Afterword and Acknowledgments

The *Adventures of Captain Graves* is the result of my love for adventure stories and tales of the sea. *The Reaper's Scythe* and this book were inspired by several sources. First and foremost, *The Reaper's Scythe* is a doppelganger of the *Zaca*, first owned by Templeton Crocker whose book, *Cruise of the Zaca* (1936) is recommended reading alongside William Beebe's *Zaca Venture* (1938). During the 1930s the *Zaca* was clearly the world's foremost exploration vessel. The *Zaca's* adventures were truncated by World War II. When Errol Flynn purchased the *Zaca* in the mid-40s he set in motion another series of adventures that are well known by Flynn's many fans.

It should be stated that this is not a fictional rendering of those adventuresome men. Captain Graves is not Errol Flynn, Templeton Crocker or William Beebe. Captain Graves is Captain Graves, and this book is entirely the work of my fevered imagination.

I am indebted to Ron Fortier and Rob Davis at Airship 27 for taking me on board. Their sterling efforts in the New Pulp literary community have set the standard for thrills and excitement. Their participation in the book adds a high level of quality for which I am forever grateful. I also owe a debt of gratitude to Ted Hammond for his stunning cover artwork, and to Ed Catto for his amazing interior illustrations. Ron, Rob, Ted and Ed, I salute you! Finally, my wife has always been my cheerleader and I am truly fortunate to have her at my side.

Credit is also due those many pulp writers who regaled their readers with tales of the sea, lost treasures and forgotten civilizations. Writers like Talbot Mundy and H. Bedford Jones are being re-discovered thanks to a growing interest in classic pulp fiction.

I also found inspiration in James A. Michener's books *Tales of the South Pacific* and *Hawaii* in addition to his television show, *Adventures in Paradise* starring the late great Gardner Mackay. Herman Melville, a long-time favorite, is a constant source of inspiration for me. Credit is due as well to Robert Louis Stevenson and Joseph Conrad. Jack London's *The Cruise of the Snark* is yet another inspiration.

Most of the paperbacks, films, automobiles and historical references mentioned in *Captain Graves* are accurate for the period. If my research has erred, then I am responsible for the error and ask the reader to indulge my fantasy and suspend their disbelief if certain historical elements are slightly out of sequence. I have also taken liberties with the history of the lady pirate, Zheng Shi.

The Adventures of Captain Graves was written as if it might have appeared in a pulp magazine in serial form, and as stories once were, with adventure itself the force behind the narrative. The framing sequence was born from my love of history and to demonstrate how swiftly Time's passage marks us all. This story is presented in the spirit of all storytellers sitting about a campfire with an audience that is eager to hear a good yarn. Should we find ourselves under those circumstances, this is the tale that I would tell. I trust that you will find it satisfactory.

Thomas McNulty
Crystal Lake, Illinois

ABOUT OUR CREATORS

AUTHOR -

THOMAS McNULTY - was born in Chicago and is a graduate of the famed writing program at Columbia College. His celebrity interviews, articles, essays, book reviews, film reviews and Hollywood and literary profiles have appeared in numerous magazines including *American Cowboy, Filmfax, The Big Reel, Classic Images, Films of the Golden Age, Kung-Fu Magazine, Mystery News, Comic Effect, Scary Monsters, The Strand Magazine On-Line* and *The Golden Gazette* among others. His celebrity interviews included actors and directors Douglas Fairbanks, Jr., Tom Hanks, John Agar, Jackie Chan, Noel Neill, Jack Elam, Burt Kennedy, David Carradine, Jeff Corey, Sheb Wooley, Vincent Sherman, Sam Mendes, Robert Vaughn, and more.

His non-fiction books include the biography *Errol Flynn* and *Werewolves! A Study of Lycanthropes in Film, Folklore and Literature.* Tom's first western adventure novel *Trail of the Burned Man* was followed by *Wind Rider, Death Rides a Palomino, Showdown at Snakebite Creek, Gunfight at Crippled Horse, Coffin for an Outlaw,* and *The Gunsmoke Serenade.*

Tom's *Jack Ripcord* is the first novel in a proposed trilogy. *Jack Ripcord* is part of the New Pulp Fiction literary movement. The phrase "New Pulp" refers to an organized group of writers and artists who are creating novels and stories in the style of the classic pulp fiction tales of the 20s, 30s and 40s.

Tom made his screen debut as an extra playing a "bank clerk" in the film *Road to Perdition* (2002), starring Tom Hanks and Paul Newman. He also interviewed and photographed the *Road to Perdition* cast for a series of magazine articles. He was a research contributor to the documentary *The Adventures of Errol Flynn,* for Top Hat Productions which aired on Turner Classic Movies. He was also a contributor to the documentary *Tasmanian Devil: The Fast and Furious Life of Errol Flynn,* for BBC Australia; and he provided the audio commentary for the Warner Brothers DVD release of *Rocky Mountain* starring Errol Flynn. And finally, Tom can be seen on the TV Land program, *Myths & Legends,* as a guest commentator. Tom's episode is titled, "Curses, Corpses and Alice Cooper."

An avid reader and bookhound, Tom regularly promotes the work of other authors on his blog "Dispatches From the Last Outlaw." He is an outspoken proponent for the advancement of literacy. Tom's other interests include comic book collecting, vintage paperback collecting, target shooting (with guns of the Old West), guitar playing, fishing and the martial arts (Tom has a Black Belt in Kyuki-Do). He lives in Crystal Lake, Illinois with his lovely wife, Jan, and a dog named Bandit.

For more information, visit Tom's blog:
"Dispatches from the Last Outlaw"
http://tommcnulty.blogspot.com

INTERIOR ILLUSTRATOR

ED CATTO - A voracious reader, Ed has been enjoying pulps since stumbling across Shadow and Doc Savage reprints as a kid. His love for illustration and art has guided him through a life-long love of comics, pulps and illustrated paperbacks. As a branding and advertising executive, Ed's career has evolved to include a focus on entertainment marketing in many ways:

A founding partner of Bonfire Agency, Ed helped establish the world's first marketing firm focused on connecting brands, in authentic ways, to passionate and enthusiastic fans of comics, graphic novels, games and movies.

Ed has also shepherded the rebirth of the iconic 60s toy, Captain Action, in collectibles, books, comics and even a national toy line. An animated television series is currently being shopped for development.

A convention enthusiast, Ed helped develop Reed Pop's New York Comic-Con (now the nation's largest con) and is currently doing the same for Syracuse's Salt City Comic-Con.

Ed speaks nationally as a panelist and moderator at conventions, leading conversations on entertainment marketing and comics history. Ed has also appeared on CNBC's Squawkbox, BNN Business News Network , and PBS's Superheroes documentary.

Ed recently started teaching at Ithaca College, sharing his experiences and enthusiasm for business and entrepreneurship to both MBA's and undergraduates. As an artist, Ed also leads graphic novel classes for kids of all ages. The Adventures of Captain Graves Marks Ed's debut as an illustrator for publisher Airship27. Ed and his wife Kathe currently live in New York's State's Finger Lakes Region, enjoying the area's local comic book shops and wineries. Between consulting, teaching and drawing, Ed continues to work very hard to whittle down the teetering tower of books on his nightstand.

COVER ARTIST

TED HAMMOND - is a Canadian artist who has been creating amazing art for over twenty years. His work has appeared in magazines, ads, books and graphic novels just to name a few. Go to (www.tedhammond.com) to contact him and check out more of his work!

TALES OF THE SOUTH SEAS

In the middle of the South Seas is the island of Motugra, so named by the natives. It has the only deep water port in this island chain. On Motugra you'll find *THE HANGING MONKEY*, an inn and bar owned and operated by Irish expatriate Corky O'Brian. Here gather some of the most colorful rogues, scalawags and pirates ever to ply the trade routes of the Pacific during the late 1930s.

Enter and meet Khuna, the bar's bouncer and former headhunter. Miko, the slim and beautiful Chinese girl with the mysterious past. One eyed Captain Nick Fortune, owner of the schooner *Fortune's Folly* and air freight pilot, Jimmy Dolan. And don't forget ace reporter, the lovely blond Grace Thomas. All of these characters spring from the mind of writer Bill Craig as homage to the classic pulp island stories of yesterday.

Here are fast-paced, island adventures guaranteed to whisk your imagination to tropical paradises of warm breezes, swaying palm trees and crystal blue waters. Where danger can lurk behind the smile of an alluring native girl and a man's fists are as important as his wits. So hitch up your gunbelt, cock your pilot's cap and swing the doors open...Welcome to The Hanging Monkey!

AN AIRSHIP 27 PRODUCTION

NEW **PULP**

airship27hangar.com